IN BED WITH THE BOSS

He's successful, powerful and extremely
sexy. He also happens to be her boss!
Used to getting his own way, he'll demand
what he wants from her—in the boardroom
and the bedroom....

Watch the sparks fly as these couples
work together—and play together!

Don't miss any of the stories in this month's
collection!

JULIE COHEN was born in the U.S.A. and brought up in the mountains of western Maine. There wasn't much going on in Maine, so she made stuff up. She spent most of her childhood with her nose in a book. After gaining her first degree in English literature, she moved to England and researched fairies in children's literature for a postgraduate degree. She started writing her first Harlequin romance novel on a blueberry farm in Maine, and finished it on a beach in Greece. Shortly after being named a finalist in the Romance Writers of America's Golden Heart contest, she sold her first novel to Harlequin® Books.

Julie lives in the south of England with her husband, who works in the music industry, and still reads everything in sight. Her other hobbies include walking, traveling, listening to loud music, watching films and eating far too much popcorn. She teaches secondary-school English and is teased daily about her American accent. Visit her Web site at www.julie-cohen.com, and write to her at julie-cohen@ntlworld.com.

MISTRESS IN PRIVATE

JULIE COHEN

~ IN BED WITH THE BOSS ~

TORONTO • NEW YORK • LONDON
AMSTERDAM • PARIS • SYDNEY • HAMBURG
STOCKHOLM • ATHENS • TOKYO • MILAN • MADRID
PRAGUE • WARSAW • BUDAPEST • AUCKLAND

ISBN-13: 978-0-373-82075-7
ISBN-10:   0-373-82075-5

MISTRESS IN PRIVATE

First North American Publication 2008.

Previously published in the U.K. under the title
ALL WORK AND NO PLAY....

www.eHarlequin.com

Printed in U.S.A.

MISTRESS
IN PRIVATE

For Kathy Love, who helped me make up
this story on a train from New York to
Washington, D.C.
I laughed so hard, I don't think I breathed
from Pennsylvania to Delaware.

CHAPTER ONE

I AM absolutely fine, I am very good at my job, and you are never going to see me cry again.

It was Jane's inner monologue, her mantra for the morning, so strong that she had to choose her words carefully to avoid speaking it out loud as she finished up her slide presentation and answered questions on behalf of her creative team.

Particularly because the person who was asking the most questions was Gary Kaplan, the senior account manager, whom she had believed she was going to marry next June, and who had seen her crying five days before.

'Fortunately for our time schedules,' she continued, clicking off her slide show and shutting down her laptop, 'the model we've selected for the Franco cologne campaign is available this week, so we're starting production straight away. I'll be seeing him and his agent for lunch after I have my design team briefing.'

'Excellent.' Allen Pearce, one of the advertising agency's partners, smiled as he rose from his chair. 'I have every confidence that my team will do the firm proud while Michael and I are in New York. Good work, Jane, Gary, and everyone.'

She'd pulled it off. She thanked Allen Pearce, thanked her team, and packed up her laptop to go back to her office. Five minutes would be enough to take a few deep breaths, compose herself, enjoy her success.

'Jane.'

Jane stopped on her way out of the boardroom. It was Gary who'd called her back, so she made sure her expression was cheerful before she turned around.

'Yes, Gary?'

'Are you all right?'

Stephen and Hasan were still gathering their things from the boardroom table, so she pretended that Gary's question was a casual enquiry.

'Fine, thanks, Gary. And you?'

She hadn't thought that her voice betrayed any of her emotions, but she did notice that Stephen and Hasan pulled together their papers and pens more quickly and headed for the door. Hasan caught her eye as he left and gave her half a smile, which, she thought, sickeningly, was probably sympathetic.

Once the other members of the team were gone, she stepped all the way back into the room and closed the door. The board-room was, like every room in Pearce Grey Advertising Agency, ultra-modern and minimalist, with white walls and grey stream-lined furniture. Sometimes she found the blank space conducive to creativity, but right now she found it cold.

Gary was still sitting in one of the sleek chairs. His crease-less grey suit fitted right into the room. She wondered if Gary was doing his own ironing, or if Kathleen lived up to his exacting standards in that department, too.

'Gary, I would appreciate it if you wouldn't ask me personal questions in front of our colleagues.' She stayed standing.

'It wasn't a personal question. I just asked you how you were doing.'

Jane used to admire Gary's calm demeanour. Now it made her hands curl up into fists. She did it behind her back, though, because one entire wall of the boardroom was glass, looking out into the main office area of Pearce Grey.

'In this context, it was a personal question,' she said.

'I asked the bloke in the newsagent the same thing this morning.'

Yes, but you didn't leave the bloke in the newsagent for another woman. 'I'm fine, Gary, thank you. How are you?'

'I'm concerned that you're not well. You look tired.'

'Isn't it odd, Gary, that when we were together you never noticed when I was tired and not well?'

He had the good sense to look uncomfortable at that question. 'Well, we weren't working so closely before your promotion.'

Which also reminded her that he had seniority. How considerate of him.

'We need you on top form,' he continued. 'The Giovanni Franco cologne campaign is vital to the agency—'

'And Giovanni Franco himself is edgy and difficult, and has sacked their last three agencies, and wants everything done yesterday,' she finished for him. 'I know. I'm on top of it.'

But then she thought about Hasan's half-smile, and how he and Stephen had hustled it out of the boardroom. Maybe she wasn't hiding her feelings as well as she'd thought.

Gary rested his arms on the desk in front of him. He was handsome enough, with light brown hair and regular features and a body that saw a gym regularly. Once upon a time he'd been a great catch for her.

'I'm wondering if it's time we let people know about our— you know.' A flicker of guilt passed across Gary's face.

She crossed her arms. 'You said it would be up to me when we told the rest of Pearce Grey we'd split up.'

'Yes, but…I think it might be easier for you if we made it public sooner rather than later. We wouldn't have to worry about how it appeared to other people.'

Jane glanced through the boardroom window at the busy office outside. It wasn't as if she and Gary had ever been demonstrative at work. But their engagement was common knowledge, and people did, she supposed, expect them to have a certain familiarity and intimacy in the way they behaved with each other.

'You mean it would be easier for you,' she said. 'You could talk about your new relationship all you liked.'

While she would be regarded with pity as the scorned fiancée. The woman who'd landed a promotion and promptly been dumped on her backside.

'It's not time yet,' she said. 'Excuse me, I have work to do.'

She left the boardroom and headed for her office, avoiding the glances of the other people who worked for the agency. She really could have used those five minutes before she had to go to her lunch meeting. Even three minutes would have been enough, a breath of time where she could look in her email inbox, see the message that Jonny had probably sent her this morning from up in the Lake District. A message from Jonny would make her smile for real.

But the design team were already gathering outside her office door. Which meant she'd be lucky to have thirty seconds to herself before she had to leave for her lunch meeting.

Jane put on a bright expression. Her email, and a real smile, would have to wait. 'Is everyone ready?' she asked.

'Jonny. Yo, Jonny.'

Jonny pushed his glasses up his nose and narrowed his eyes, forcing himself to concentrate on the HTML code on the laptop screen in front of him. Thom's voice wasn't easy to ignore. It was loud, vibrant, and unabashedly Californian. Jonny typed in a line of code anyway.

'Jonathan Richard Cole Junior!' Thom leaned across the first-class railway carriage table and waved his hand in Jonny's face.

Jonny gave up and looked at his friend. 'In case you hadn't noticed, I was ignoring you. I gave you one condition for this trip when you kidnapped me, remember?'

'I didn't kidnap you, dude!' Thom put on his fake-innocent grin. 'I let you go get your computer and a toothbrush before I dragged you to the Penrith train station. And I only came up to get you in person because I know what you're like when you're writing a book.'

Jonny smiled, because it was impossible to stay annoyed with Thom Erikson. The man was incredibly rich, incredibly generous, and he talked as if he had a surfboard permanently attached to his person. And he'd stayed close to Jonny, even when Jonny had left California to go back to England.

In a world full of transitions and disillusion, Jonny had learned to appreciate loyalty, even when the loyalty was also accompanied by unrelenting persistence.

'You also agreed not to call me by my real name,' Jonny

reminded him. 'When I'm working with you I'm not Jonny Cole, I'm Jay Richard.'

'Oh, yeah. I forgot because you had your Clark Kent glasses on. Sorry.'

Clark Kent. Jonny took off his glasses and rubbed his nose, thinking that comparison wasn't so far-fetched. He didn't become a Superman when he took his glasses off, but his life certainly got different.

He'd prefer leaping tall buildings to posing in front of cameras, though.

'I wish you'd change your mind about the pseudonym,' Thom continued. 'Your double life would make great publicity: computer how-to guru moonlights as one of Britain's most up-and-coming male models. From geek to gorgeous. Dweeb to dude. Nerd to—'

'Enough.' Jonny laughed, holding up his hands. 'I'm not going to use my real job to get myself publicity, because as soon as I make enough money I'm quitting modelling. I told you that when I started.'

'You are so deluded, my man. You're a natural and the camera loves you. You could have a very, very good career in modelling. And this new job is a real triumph. The face of Giovanni Franco's new cologne.' Thom whistled.

Jonny did have to concede that Thom should know what he was talking about. The man ran one of the most successful modelling agencies on the west coast of the USA, so successful he'd started to branch into Europe.

And Jonny also had to admit that, much as he disliked the idea of being a model, it was a godsend right now.

'I didn't have an easy time of it as a teenager,' he told Thom. 'I really was a computer geek then. I only started working out so I could fight back against the guys who used to beat me up on a regular basis.'

'And success is the best revenge, right?'

Jonny shook his head. 'The situation hasn't changed. I'm still being judged by my appearance. Ultimately, it's not honest. I'm not a body, I'm a…bloke. I'm a writer. I'm me.

That's why I want to keep my modelling life and my real life separate. And then when I've made enough money, it's back to the writing.'

'Dude.' Thom leaned forward again. 'If you need money, I'll write you a cheque. You don't need to face a single camera. You know that.'

'No,' Jonny said, and then realised he'd said it violently enough to make his friend blink. 'I mean, thank you, Thom. But I'll earn my money.'

'What do you need so much money for, anyway? If you're in trouble—'

'I'll be all right,' Jonny said, and, although he didn't want to hurt Thom's feelings, he said it crisply enough to stop the discussion.

Thom was a Californian, and Californians talked about everything. Despite Jonny's own years on the west coast of America, he was still English, and he still knew that some things were best kept private.

A woman came down the train aisle with a trolley of coffee and tea. They gave it to you free in first class, a fact Jonny never would have discovered without Thom and his insistence on travelling the best way possible. 'Coffee, thanks,' Jonny said when she stopped at their seats, and his eyes wandered back to his laptop. When the coffee didn't arrive, he looked up.

The woman was staring at him, half a smile on her face. She was cute, with blonde hair scraped back into a pony-tail. Her cheeks flushed slightly as she said, 'I'm sorry, I don't usually ask things like this, but haven't I seen you somewhere before?'

'Now that you ask, Jay's been in—'

Jonny interrupted before Thom could start on the list of magazines and advertisements he'd got Jonny jobs modelling for. 'I don't think we've met, no. Sorry.'

The woman looked from Jonny's polite smile to Thom's grin, and then back to Jonny. 'Oh. Well, here's your coffee, and if I can get you anything else…' Her voice, though shy, was unmistakably flirtatious.

'Just the coffee is fine, thank you.'

Thom snagged a can of cola as the trolley passed, and settled back in his seat, shaking his head sadly. 'You disappoint me, my friend. That was your perfect chance. Stewardesses are hot.'

'She wasn't a stewardess. This is a train, not a plane.'

Thom leaned out into the aisle and looked after the woman. 'Uniform is still pretty cute from behind, though.' He turned back to Jonny. 'Do you know how many women are hot for models? And how many of those models are actually straight? You're a rarity and you should be shagging everything in sight.'

'Thom, I want to hook up with a woman because I have something in common with her, not because she's seen me in some magazine.'

'You mean you want a female computer geek.' Thom took a long drink of his cola. 'That's fortunate, because, with the amount of time you spend on a computer, I bet the only sex you're getting is virtual.'

'You know, Thom, I'd be much more offended by what you're saying if I didn't personally know that you haven't had sex since the last leap year.'

'We're not talking about me. We're talking about you. You're living up in the middle of nowhere and you spend all your time online. When we get to London, how about I set you up with somebody?'

'That won't be necessary. I'm meeting somebody already.'

Like his evasion of Thom's questions about his financial situation, this wasn't quite the whole truth, and Jonny felt a stab of guilt. It was a measure of how much the circumstances of the past few months had affected him that he was being deliberately misleading.

'I mean, I'm going to try to meet a friend,' he corrected himself. 'You didn't give me a whole lot of notice that I was coming to London.'

'A friend.' Thom looked interested. 'Is this a sex friend?'

'No. She's a friend. I've known her since I was a kid, but we fell out of touch, and we only started emailing each other a few months ago when I got back to England and found her on the web. She lives in London.'

'A virtual girlfriend. How do you do that whole cyber-sex

thing? I never really understood it. Do you, like, describe what you're doing to each other, and then use toys, or—?'

Jonny had to laugh at Thom's single-mindedness. 'We're not having cyber sex. I used to have a huge crush on her, but that was when we were kids. I haven't seen her since we were about eleven years old. And she's engaged. She's just—'

He tried to think of how to describe it. Jane was his friend, but it was more than that. Even though they'd never met up, over the past few months Jane's emails had been just about the only thing that kept him sane.

'She's got a great sense of humour, and we seem to have a lot in common. We email four or five times a day.'

'Oh.' Thom's playful interest had been replaced by something more serious. 'She's the one you tell things to, huh?'

The one you tell things to. Yeah, he wished. How many times had he sat down and written to Jane, typed all of his problems and worries and disillusion into the computer to send to her…and then deleted the whole thing before he sent it?

It was too painful to say. Even not out loud, even to someone he didn't see in person. Even to someone he cared about.

'Anyway,' he said, 'she's got a fiancé, so there's never going to be anything between us.'

'Man, you've got to be crazy. There is no way her fiancé is as good-looking as you. You just snap your fingers, she'll drop at your feet.'

'Thom,' Jonny said warningly.

'Okay, okay. I was just saying. I get it, you're deeper than that and you're a decent guy who doesn't break up relationships. I think you're insane, but that's nothing new. You do like her despite the fiancé, though, right? Tell Uncle Thom.'

'I've wanted to marry her since I was nine,' Jonny admitted. 'But I'll settle for dinner—if you give me any time off from posing for a camera.'

Thom pulled out his palm organiser and began tapping through it. 'Well, we've got shoots scheduled for most of the day on Wednesday, Thursday, and Friday, but you should have some time free in the evening to meet your lady friend.'

'And to do my real work. I've got a deadline for a book in three weeks. *HTML for Utter Beginners.*'

'And to play. There are some mega parties you need to go to, especially mine on Friday. First, though, you and I are having lunch with the creative director from Pearce Grey, the advertising agency who's hired you for the Franco campaign. Her name's Jane Miller. You'll like her.'

At the name, Jonny sat up straighter and smothered a chuckle.

He knew Jane Miller. And he definitely liked her.

In fact, he'd wanted to marry her since he was nine.

'Sounds perfect,' he said, pushing his glasses back on and clicking open his email program on his laptop. He'd already emailed Jane once today, this morning before he'd caught the train, but this called for another message.

'Just one thing, Jonny?'

'Mmm?'

'Put in your contact lenses before we get to London, or I'll call you Clark Kent by mistake.'

'No problem,' said Jonny, and started to type.

Subject: Today
Hey Jane, remember I said I was coming to London if you wanted to meet up? Turns out we're meeting after all. I have something to confess to you: I'm moonlighting as a model, and you've got a lunch date today with my agent Thom Erikson and me.

He smiled. It felt good to come clean about his double life to someone else.

He glanced over at Thom, who was absorbed in his organiser again.

Jonny remembered Jane as a kid. She'd been vibrant, exciting and full of adventure, as outgoing as her four older brothers. She'd looked like a naughty porcelain doll, with her long wavy hair and her sparkling grey eyes.

Jane was up for a little bit of intrigue. She could keep this secret; in fact, she'd probably think it was fun.

Thing is, when I'm modelling, I'm known as Jay Richard instead of Jonny Cole. When we're with other people, would you mind calling me Jay? It sounds weird, but I'll explain it to you when we get a minute by ourselves. Looking forward to seeing you again. Love, Jonny.

As he hit the send button, he wondered if Jane Miller was still as adventurous as she used to be.

He hoped so.

Jane walked into the Covent Garden bistro and glanced around its trendy interior. She didn't see Thom Erikson, or the model she'd hired through him to be the face of Giovanni Franco's new cologne. Then again, of the two of them, she'd only met Thom in person—she'd seen the model in glossy photographs she'd gone through with her art director, so she might not recognise him in real life. From seven years of working in advertising, she knew very well that appearances didn't always reflect reality.

It was a lesson she'd been wrestling with constantly for the past week.

At least lunch would be enjoyable, she thought as the hostess led her to the table she'd reserved. She liked Thom, and it was always interesting to meet models, as long as they weren't chain smokers. They had odd quirks and they were good to look at, and Thom's models tended to have a sense of humour.

Wouldn't it just show Gary if I ended up dating a model? she thought, and snorted. She came up with crazy ideas all the time for her job, but this was probably one of the craziest. As if a model would ever notice her enough to ask her out.

Jane pulled her BlackBerry out of her briefcase, figuring she might as well use the time as she waited for Thom and Jay Richard. This morning had been hard work; she deserved a minute or two to look for an email from Jonny.

Her machine took a moment to connect, and when she looked up a man was smiling at her.

He had dark hair and he wore a loose white shirt, unbuttoned at the cuffs. His hands were in the pockets of his faded jeans.

He stood casually, comfortably, looking straight at her, and his eyes were dark blue. Even across the room she could see it.

Jane's fingers gripped her BlackBerry hard. This was her model. It must be, he looked so familiar. But, somehow, in a different way than she'd expected. It wasn't like recognising someone from a photo. The sight of him connected inside her stomach, making her joints ache and her breasts tighten. Her tailored suit stifled her, felt too tight across her chest.

He had perfect teeth, sculpted lips, high cheekbones, and he wasn't just smiling at her, he was beaming.

Jane couldn't help it. She flicked her head to the side, looking over her shoulder to see who was behind her, because men this gorgeous did not *beam* at her.

When she looked back he was striding across the restaurant, nearly at her table, his hand outstretched.

And then he was there. In front of her, holding her hand in his, though she didn't remember offering it.

'Jane,' he said, his head tilted slightly to the side, his smile digging creases into the side of his mouth. His voice was deep, soft, and friendly.

The sound of her name in his mouth did something to her blood because she felt as if she had too much of it, heating her skin, pumping her heart harder, tingling in her fingertips and chest.

'Yes.' She stood on weak legs, hearing her voice shaky and realising, somewhere in the back of her boiling brain, that she should really try to control her behaviour before she made herself look like an idiot. But this man…

'You look different from your photographs,' she said.

'I really hope so,' he said, and the warmth in his eyes and his hand made her swallow, hard.

'Dude, you found her!'

A man in a white linen suit burst out of nowhere. He clapped the gorgeous man on the shoulder and kissed Jane on both of her cheeks. 'Hey, Jane, great to see you, babe. I see you know Jay already.'

'Thom,' she said, in confusion, and then realised that she was still holding the model's hand. 'It's great to meet you, Jay,' she said, giving his hand a shake, trying to inject some professionalism into the gesture that was, for her, quite frankly sensual.

His hand enfolded hers, warm and dry, and it was as if she could feel every line of his palm, every print of his fingertips against her. It was more than a handshake. She felt as if she *knew* him.

She met his eyes again and he was smiling as if he shared a secret with her.

He knew. He knew he made her feel this way.

'I'm glad to meet you too, Jane,' he said, and his voice was knowing, too. 'It looks as if we interrupted your emailing.' He glanced down at her BlackBerry, where her emails had loaded.

'Oh, not at all,' she said, dropping his hand at last and scooping up her BlackBerry to close it down. She couldn't help glance back up at his face, though, and when she did, he winked at her.

Winked. As if they were already friends, as if he were flirting with her. He stepped behind her and pulled out her seat for her—not that she needed it, she had just stood up—and before she could sink into it, he whispered, 'You look even better than I thought you would.'

Oh-h-h. She got it, now. He was a charmer, someone who thought that his good looks gave him the right to flatter and flirt with every woman.

'Thank you,' she said, and if her attraction to him meant that she couldn't quite inject her reply with the requisite coolness, he seemed to understand some of it, because he retreated to the other side of the table and sat down next to Thom.

Her body was disappointed. Her body, traitor that it was, wanted Jay to sit next to her and stay close to her. Her mind, however, registered that if she was sitting across from him, she'd be able to look at him for the entire meal, which was quite bad enough.

'Jay's very excited to be working on the Franco campaign with you,' Thom was saying, and if it hadn't been so weird she would have sworn that Thom dug an elbow into Jay's side. 'Aren't you, Jay?'

'Very,' he said, and he caught Jane's eye again. Jane couldn't figure it out. It was as if he were trying to communicate some other message to her, something beyond the normal chit-chat of a professional meeting, something even beyond what must be, for him, routine flirting.

But what else would he be trying to say?

'So how long have you been modelling, Jay?' she asked brightly.

The look he gave her was wry, almost rueful, which didn't make sense either, because if he was a charmer who relied on his looks, wouldn't he be into his modelling career?

'Not long,' he answered. 'Thom's an old friend and he conned me into it.'

'It's not my fault if the camera loves you, dude,' Thom said.

Jane dropped her gaze briefly to look at Jay's body, what she could see of it across the table. She could see why the camera loved him. He was all lean, strong lines. His clothes were comfortably loose on his body, but she could tell from the bit of chest exposed in the V of his shirt and his dark-haired forearms that he was slim, but packed with muscle.

Some models, even the male ones, were too skinny, but Jay had a body that looked good in real life, too. They'd chosen him partly because Giovanni Franco wanted somebody masculine, who looked more like a man than some of the boyish models on the catwalks.

'I'm not so sure I love the camera,' Jay was saying to Thom. 'And you only think modelling is a great profession because you haven't been forced to look brooding under hot lights for hours on end.'

She dragged her eyes away from that V of tanned skin at the base of his neck, and sat back in her seat, trying for a semblance of ease. 'Don't you think that's a fair turnaround for the years that women have been objectified by the media?' she said.

'Ha!' cried Thom. 'She's got you there, bud. You're striking a blow for feminism by being a sex object. Think of that next time you're posing in your underwear.'

Jay threw back his head and laughed, and she could see the texture of his skin. He was tanned and he hadn't shaved this morning, so a slight rough stubble shadowed his well-formed jaw and around his beautiful mouth.

She wondered what it would feel like on her neck. Under her lips.

A menu appeared in front of her and she took it without looking at the waitress who offered it. Instead, she looked at Jay's hands as they accepted the menu. They were as lean and strong as the rest of him.

He smiled at her over the menu and the pulse of desire that ripped through her was so strong that she nearly gasped.

'Would you like something to drink, some wine?' she heard a female voice say, and Jane tore her gaze away from Jay to look up at the waitress, ask for the wine menu, take charge of this situation instead of letting her libido do it for her.

And this time, she did gasp, as her body temperature went from overheated to zero.

'Oh, crap,' she said.

CHAPTER TWO

IT WAS Kathleen. Big-breasted, tousle-haired, full-lipped Kathleen.

'You're a *waitress*?' Jane said.

'Oh.' Kathleen stood stock-still, the wine list in her hand. 'This—is awkward.'

'Thom,' Jane said, her voice much calmer than she would have thought possible, 'would you mind choosing the wine? I'll be right back.'

'Sure,' she heard Thom reply, but she didn't wait to see what he thought of her behaviour. Instead she walked straight across the restaurant and into the ladies' room.

It was empty. Jane kicked the marble base of the sink. She didn't know what to do, so she washed her hands. She wished she could wash out her mouth, too. Or wash the last five minutes away.

'He left me for a *waitress*,' she said to her reflection, and then turned the water back on to wash her hands again.

She heard a soft knock on the door. 'Jane?'

She went around the sink to the door. It was open a crack, and she could see a hand and half a face. Blue-eyed, jaw rough with brown stubble. Jay.

'Jane? Are you all right?'

She sighed and opened the door all the way. Fortunately the ladies' room was in a corridor off the main dining room, so the entire restaurant couldn't witness her conversation with a male model through the lavatory door.

'I'm fine,' she said. 'I'm sorry I said "crap".'

Jay shrugged. 'I've said worse, and so has Thom. I can be quite an inventive swearer, actually. What's the matter?'

'Nothing. It's—everything is fine.' She smiled.

The expression on his face let her know she wasn't being convincing. 'Okay. Listen, Thom's sorting out the bill and getting us a table at the restaurant next door. Do you like Italian?'

Her cheeks flushed hot. Some professional she was—she was meant to be the host. 'That's not necessary, I'll be—'

'It's necessary,' Jay interrupted her. 'And don't say the word "fine" any more. I know you've got a better vocabulary than that, even when you're lying.'

His words surprised a laugh out of her. 'Okay.'

Jay rested his shoulder against the wall beside him, the same sort of casual, comfortable stance he'd had when she'd first seen him. It brought him a little bit closer to her. She'd expect a model to wear some sort of cologne, especially as he was advertising it, but he smelled of warm cotton.

'Do you want to tell me what's wrong, Jane?'

For a split second, she was tempted.

It would be a relief to tell someone what was going on. She'd kept it in and kept it in and sometimes she felt as if she were going to explode. Jay was looking at her with concern in his blue eyes, a slight furrow between his eyebrows. And he looked so damn familiar, as if she'd known this stranger all her life.

But she didn't know him.

'Did you see her shoes?' she asked instead. 'The waitress's?'

He nodded, seemingly not put off by the change in topic at all.

'Were they cheap, or expensive?' A model would know these things, she was sure.

'Cheap,' he said without hesitation. 'Needed resoling. If she stands in those all day she's headed for corns.'

Her laughter this time wasn't quite so unexpected, and it relaxed her a little bit.

'Jane,' he said, leaning closer to her, his voice lower and sincere, 'I don't know who that waitress is, but if it helps you to know this, you are about a million times prettier than she is. And you have a better job, and I'm certain you have a better personality.' His gaze dropped downward, taking her in. 'And you have much better shoes.'

Jane's skin heated, because, although he was discussing her shoes, he hadn't just looked at her feet. He'd looked at her body on the way down. Just a look, but she was pretty much melting.

Wouldn't it show Gary if I went out with a model? she thought again, and then again brushed the thought aside. She'd already mixed up her personal and her professional life, and it was a very bad idea.

'Thanks,' she said. 'I guess we'd better get back to—'

Jay touched her arm, the bare skin of her wrist, and she stopped, arrested by the feeling of his flesh on hers again.

'You're doing wonderfully, by the way,' he said. 'I appreciate it.'

That was an odd thing to say, but she supposed it was meant as some sort of encouragement. 'Thank you. I'm usually a very professional person.'

'I know.'

His fingers were still wrapped around her wrist. He could probably feel every beat of her heart. As if he were touching, somehow, her life force.

Everything about him felt as if she'd known him for so, so long, maybe in a neglected corner of her mind where she paid attention to dreams and desires.

'Will you have dinner with me tonight?' she blurted out.

She could see the mild surprise in his eyes. 'I would love to. Do you mean just the two of us, or—?'

'Just the two of us,' she replied, before she could think through what it was she had just done, or the probability that he would reject her. When she'd first started out in advertising, she'd learned to let her impulses loose, even the crazy ones, even the ones that would never work in a million years. Because sometimes they did work.

But she hadn't let her impulses loose for some time, now.

'I mean, don't worry if you don't want to, I know you're busy, and—'

'I would love to.'

That brought her up short. 'Oh.' She swallowed, put some more poise into her voice, and said, 'Well, that's wonderful. How about eight o'clock?'

'Fantastic.' His smile was both genuine and perfect. He nodded back towards the restaurant. 'Shall we go and be professional now?'

'Definitely.' She stepped through the ladies' room door and joined him, walking back across the restaurant, wondering with every step what the hell she had just got herself into.

Four and a half hours later, she was still wondering. Except this time she was pacing the living room of her high-ceilinged, brick-walled loft, wringing her hands.

Half of her was remembering Jay at lunch that afternoon. How he'd smiled when he'd said yes to her date, his hand curled intimately around her wrist. And then the rest of the meal, where they'd stuck safely to talk about modelling and the campaign and more general chat, and Jane had felt more like herself.

Except for the moments when she'd watched him eat. Knife and fork, held in his long-fingered hands. It was silly to be aroused by watching somebody cut his food. But she was. His movements were economical, the tendons on the back of his hand flexing, his fingers agile.

Whenever he took a bite of his risotto, she had to consider his mouth. How his bottom lip was fuller than the top. How both lips curved upwards at the corners, in a sexy near-smile. How white and even his teeth were.

At one point he'd licked his bottom lip and she'd almost dropped her water glass because all she could think of was his mouth on her, his tongue in her mouth, how his hair would feel under her hands as she kissed him.

And then he'd looked at her and smiled, with that somehow warm and intimate look, as if he and she shared a secret from the rest of the world.

The man was the most beautiful human being she had ever seen in her entire life and she could not work out what he thought was going on between them. Unless he gave every woman this feeling, unless he had charm down to such an art that he appeared to be sincere in the most unusual way she'd ever encountered.

And what on earth was she going to do with him tonight?

Jane stopped pacing, sat down at her desk and opened her

laptop, going straight to the Giovanni Franco cologne campaign files. She clicked on the notes her art director, Amy, had made for her when they were in the process of choosing Jay Richard as the model for the campaign. Maybe they would tell her something more about this man.

She skimmed the notes, picking up phrases as she went. 'Client wants an easygoing attitude.' 'Warm face, which customers can relate to.' Well, that was correct, and went some way to showing her that she hadn't lost her mind. 'Model not perfect, but appealing, likely to conform to image consumers would like for themselves.' Jane snorted at that one. He looked perfect enough to her.

She called up one of his portfolio photos. He was leaning with one hand on a doorframe, wearing a slim-fitting long-sleeved T-shirt that emphasised the lean lines of his body. He was smiling just enough to dig a crease in his left cheek. He looked as if he was about to start a conversation, or reach out and touch the observer.

He looked nearly exactly as he'd looked when he'd stood outside the ladies' room, talking with her.

Rationally, she knew it meant he'd been acting. But the familiar pose still made her warm, made her breath come faster.

'Oh, crap,' she moaned. 'Why did I decide it would be a good thing to date a model?'

Her laptop made a 'whishht' sound and a little box popped up in the corner of the screen to tell her that Jonny Cole had logged into the chat program they sometimes used.

He'd probably emailed her earlier; he emailed her just about every day. But she'd been so busy this morning and this afternoon after lunch that she hadn't had time to check any personal stuff, and whatever he'd sent was most likely buried in her inbox. And of course since she'd got home she'd been angsting.

But Jonny would calm her down. She opened her email application and began to scroll through messages, looking for his return address. Most of the stuff she had that wasn't work-related was spam about stock tips and enlarging her penis. How she was supposed to find the single message that actually meant something…

Her laptop chimed. A glance told her it was Jonny hailing her. She abandoned her inbox and clicked on the chat icon.

Hello gorgeous! How are you?

She could see Jonny's message appearing as he typed. Jane hadn't seen Jonny in person for fifteen years, but she could remember well what he used to look like when they were kids and he would come over to her house nearly every day to play. He'd been a skinny boy with a brown bowl cut, knobbly knees, and round glasses. He was a lot more fragile than her four older, boisterous brothers; at times, his shyness had made him seem even more fragile than Jane was herself. Jane was used to being around bigger boys, but Jonny always liked hanging around with her more than with her brothers.

Whenever she pictured him now, at twenty-seven, she thought of him as a skinny man with the same bowl cut and round glasses, sort of like a grown-up Harry Potter. He was a self-described computer geek, but she bet he was cute.

It was typical of him that he called her 'gorgeous'. Of course, he hadn't seen her in fifteen years, either.

Before she replied, Jane glanced down at herself. She wore the skirt of her brown suit, and a shell top. Her light daily make-up had probably worn off, and her plain brown hair was pulled back into a clip, as usual.

She looked businesslike. She wasn't gorgeous. She typed back:

Hey Jonny. I'm fine.

Liar.

The reply came back lightning-fast, so quickly it made her gasp in the empty room.

Jay had said nearly the same thing.

Suddenly Jane was blinking back tears. She'd fought and fought for the past few days to act as if everything was okay, as if she had no worries. She was sick of it. Surrounded all day, every day, by people who wanted her at peak efficiency, who didn't want to know how she felt, and when she came home, she was all alone. She didn't even have anywhere comfortable to sit because Gary had taken his couch.

Gary and I broke up.

She typed and sent it before she could think better of it. And then she did think better of it, and wrote the more honest truth:

Gary left me for another woman.

It was a moment before Jonny replied.

I understand. I'm sorry, Jane.

He's a bastard.

Well, that goes without saying.

And she's a waitress with bad shoes.

Again, a slight pause before Jonny wrote back.

Why does her job make a difference?

Because I've worked so hard to be a success, to be good at my job, and Gary was proud of me. He said he was proud of me. And then he leaves me for somebody who comes home every night smelling of other people's food?

As soon as she typed it, the answer felt inadequate, but she didn't think she was going to get much closer to the truth typing into a silly little box, so she sent it.

I was wondering about the shoes, but now I think I get it. You're saying she doesn't even have good taste and it feels unfair.

It's mostly because Gary wears these Italian shoes and I had some comfortable slippers I used to wear around the house and he kept on commenting about them until I had to throw them away. I've never found another pair that was so comfortable. How come it's okay for her to wear crappy shoes and I can't even keep my slippers?

Her fingers were flying over the keyboard and Jane didn't feel like crying any more. Instead, she felt lighter. It was a huge relief to say what she was thinking to somebody who wouldn't judge her and who tried to understand, even if it was via a computer and a network, even if it was to someone whom she never saw in person. She hit 'send' and started typing again immediately, without even taking a breath.

So now I've got this date tonight with this gorgeous model person and I don't know what to do.

It's a date?

Jonny's reply came back fast as thought.

Yes. And I don't know what to do.

Excuse me for a moment, while I run around the room whooping in joy.

Jane laughed out loud. She loved Jonny's sense of humour, and it was typical of him that he was so happy for her that she had a date.

Okay, I'm back. I think I scared the neighbours. So what do you mean, you don't know what to do?

Jane sighed.

I haven't dated for ages. I'm not sure how you behave. Even with Gary, we didn't really date...we were working

*together and we just sort of got together. I'm not sure I
know what to do with a man.*

I'm sure you know perfectly well.

She glanced down at herself again. Plain Jane, career woman
with no social life. She couldn't even keep a man faithful to her
when she was engaged to him.

She understood men, she thought. She'd grown up with four
brothers, after all. Most of her colleagues at work were male.
She'd always thought that men were refreshing, because they
usually said what they meant, and the motivations for their
actions were usually pretty clear.

But when it came to relationships, she obviously didn't have
a clue. Because she'd thought that everything with Gary was
fine, right up until the minute he'd introduced her to his new girlfriend. She wrote:

*I don't know what men like in a woman. I'm not sure
what they think is sexy, or what they'd like a woman to
do on a date.*

She pressed 'send', and then, in one of her impulses, her
second today, she typed:

Tell me what to do, Jonny. Tell me what you would like.

Jonny stared at the screen and swallowed.

Had he stepped into some strange virtual world, or was this
one of his fantasies coming true?

Jane Miller was wonderful, beautiful, intriguing. It had been
fifteen years and she was all grown up, and he'd recognised her
the minute he'd walked into the restaurant. Even though her hair
was pulled back neatly into a clip, the strands that escaped were
still as thick and soft and wavy as he remembered. Her eyes were

big and grey, her lips were a perfect bow, and her skin was as delicate as the petal of an orchid.

He hadn't just recognised her with his eyes and his mind; he'd recognised her with his heart, as the girl he'd followed around and adored for years when he was a kid. She'd been a crush, yeah, the untouchable girl he'd dreamed unformed pre-adolescent dreams about, but she'd also been his friend. She was still his friend.

And he'd recognised her with his body, too. Because Jane had grown from a tomboy into a very attractive woman.

He'd barely been able to keep his hands off her. His first instinct when he'd seen her had been to sweep her into his arms and plant an enormous kiss on those doll-like lips. It was attraction, it was affection, and it was also a primitive urge to grab this woman and mark her as his, because he'd always wanted her to be.

But there had been her fiancé to consider, and Thom, and the charade he'd asked her to play.

And now…

This was a real date. Just the two of them. Two grown-ups, both of them single.

And she was asking him what he would like to happen. He replied carefully.

What do you mean?

I mean everything. What should I wear, for example?

Jonny closed his eyes and took a deep breath.

She'd been wearing a suit at lunch this afternoon, and it had been pretty modest, nondescript in colour, conservative in cut. It was probably designed to minimise her femininity, but Jonny wasn't fooled by it. He'd looked closely enough to see the slender curve of her waist under her jacket, the wave of her hips under her skirt, the slight bounce of her breasts under her silky top.

And the graceful line of her neck, and the delicacy of her wrists, slim and throbbing with warmth under his palm when he'd touched her.

And her shoes. Her suit had been nondescript, but her shoes had been fine leather, high-heeled, and had made her legs go on for ever. He typed:

You have good shoes. You should wear heels. They're very sexy.

I should definitely wear good shoes. What else?

A dress. Something that doesn't hide your body.

High heels and a clingy dress. Got it. Should I wear fancy underwear? Forget it, don't answer that, of course I should.

Jonny nearly fell off his chair.

'What colour?' he asked aloud, his voice hoarse, but didn't type it. Instead, he pictured it. White lace on that porcelain skin. Black satin hugging the curves of her buttocks. Pink silk pushing up her sweet breasts, barely covering her nipples.

He didn't care what colour, actually. His blood had rushed to his crotch and he was sporting a hard-on of epic proportions.

If he spent the entire date knowing Jane was wearing fancy underwear just for him, he was going to have difficulty standing up and walking without attracting attention.

Okay, so how should I behave?

The ding of Jane's message broke him out of his reverie, though it couldn't distract him completely.

Just be yourself, Jane. No man could ask for more.

You're very sweet, Jonny, but I need more information. Should I be flirtatious? Seductive? How do I do it?

The thoughts about Jane's underwear didn't go away, but he also remembered her at lunch today. He hadn't been able to take his eyes off her. Jane had tried to act normally, talking with Thom, pretending to study the menu and appreciate her food—but he'd caught her attention wandering back to him, again and again. She'd looked in his eyes just a little too long when they'd spoken to each other; she'd cast quick, fluttering glances at his body.

Since he'd started modelling he'd become used to glances like that from women, but Jane was different. Every glance from her had heated his skin with desire—and, more than that, her eyes on him had made him feel like laughing out loud with happiness.

The mutual attraction between them was the best thing that had happened to him for a very long time. He typed:

I mean it. Just be yourself. You're seductive without any help.

And you're not BEING any help, Jonny. I need to know how to be sexy. What would you think if a woman did something like leaning forward on the table to mistakenly/ deliberately show you her cleavage? Or is that too tacky?

Jonny swallowed. Jane Miller, the girl of his dreams, deliberately leaning forward in her clingy dress, showing him her cleavage in her 'fancy underwear'...

That would work.

What else? I'm bad at this, remember. Tell me what you like.

Oh, dear Lord. Jonny took a deep breath, closed his eyes, and typed without looking at the laptop, because his inner vision behind his eyelids was showing Jane, doing every little thing she could do to turn him on.

Cross your legs, let your skirt ride up a little, laugh, lean back in your chair. Wear your hair loose and twist a strand of it around your finger. Reach out, with small touches, a stroke on my arm or hand. Throw back your head in that adventurous way that you have. Get close, let us breathe the same air. Let your eyes show how you feel.

He opened his eyes only to press 'send', and he watched his words appear in the dialogue box.

In black-and-white, the words looked different than they had in his head. Starker. More like orders, rather than fantasy.

His heart rate sped up, partly with anxiety, but mostly with excitement. His blood pounded through his body and heated his limbs and made his erection pulse in his trousers.

His adventurous Jane, the fearless girl who climbed trees and jumped into pools of water without looking first. Was she playing with him, teasing him? Was she really as uncertain as she said?

She'd made the first move by asking him out, and now she was taking it further before they even met again, and either motivation appealed to him. He could play with her or he could reassure her. Or he could do both. He could tell her what he wanted from her, as he'd never done with any other woman before, because what he wanted most from her was that she be herself.

Unless, of course, she didn't like what he'd written.

The seconds stretched into minutes. Jonny shifted in his seat, adjusting the fit of his trousers. The hotel-room chair wasn't all that comfortable, especially for a desperately turned on man glued to his laptop. He pictured Jane sitting in her flat, reading the words he'd written, picturing the two of them together, maybe her brow furrowed a little, thinking about what she would do.

He raised his hands to the keyboard to ask if she was still there, but then saw that she was typing, and her answer appeared.

Okay. I can do that. But I have another question. What do you think about kissing?

A sound escaped Jonny's throat, half a laugh, half a gasp of surprise.

I like it a lot.

His mouth was in a wide smile as he typed, his head shaking in disbelief that he was having this conversation online.

But what about a first kiss? What should it be like? Should it be all chaste and sweet, or should there be tongues involved? Do you just promise something, or do you really get into it and get all passionate? What do you think?

I rather think it might depend on the circumstances.

Jonny was actually breathless as he typed, he noticed with the part of his brain that was still rational. He continued:

You know, what feels right at the time.

He hit 'send', and then couldn't help typing:

Personally I like passion. What do you want out of a first kiss, Jane?

The answer came back in seconds.

I want it all.

He had to stand up and walk around the room, because those four words on his screen made him feel as if he wanted to explode, as if he didn't want to wait for eight o'clock and seeing Jane in the restaurant, but instead get a cab straight to her address and when she answered the door grab her and give her a kiss that had all the passion she could ever want.

When he typed, his hands were shaking slightly.

You can have it all, Jane.

And do you think we should have sex with each other?

He could barely respond.

Do you want to?

You know, I think I do.

Jonny didn't move or breathe. He was normally a visual person, but the fantasy that filled his mind wasn't just a picture. It was a full-body imagining of what it would feel like to have Jane's smooth, bare skin against his. How her breasts and hips would feel under his hands, the gasp she would make as he touched her. The weight of her leg twined around his as they lay together. A soft giggle in his ear. Her mouth, soft as petals, her little hands stroking up his back. And the wet, tight heat inside her.

He groaned aloud.

Tell me one more thing, Jonny, just for information, and then I'll leave you in peace for now. What's your wildest fantasy?

He was being driven insane by desire and he typed furiously, without slowing down to let his brain think about what he was communicating.

We can't wait for dinner to be over. We get up and leave together and when we're outside, in the cool spring air, we immediately touch each other. We slide our hands inside each other's clothing and we touch whatever skin we can, kissing and exploring and not caring about the other people walking past us in the evening. Our clothes are in the way but that's exciting, too, because every touch promises even more.

He pressed 'send' and kept on typing without a break.

And we're laughing, Jane, and we hail a taxi and go to the closest possible place where we fall through the door and pull our clothes aside, don't even bother to take them off, and have the hottest sex in the world up against the nearest wall.

As he typed he felt it. Jane's impatient hands on his belt, pushing aside his trousers and taking hold of his erection. Him pressing her against the wall, holding her there while she wrapped her legs around his waist and he nudged aside her dress and suckled her breast, hard. Her strangled cry of pleasure. How their bodies would thrust together and how they would climax with a noise half of ecstasy, half of amazed amusement.

And then we would spend the rest of the night taking it slow, exploring, talking. Sharing and getting to know each other again.

He took a long, shaky breath, and looked back at what he had typed.

It took a moment for his eyes to focus, and then the impact of his words registered in his brain.

He'd just had cyber sex with Jane.

He lifted his hand to his mouth and bit the side of his finger. His heartbeat throbbed almost painfully even in this little piece of him. Inside his boxers, his penis was like a rod of red-hot iron, pulsing and insistent and wanting to rob him of every single bit of his intellect and conscience and modesty.

What had he just done?

She'd asked for his fantasy. Not what he'd actually planned on doing this evening, which was having a terrific date and seeing how they felt about each other. Not what he thought was probably best for them to do, which was talk about how she felt about her break-up and decide to take it easy until she very definitely wasn't on the rebound.

No. She'd asked for his wildest fantasy and he'd given it to her, including groping in public and sex up against a wall.

And she was probably about to give him the internet equivalent of a slap in the face.

He shifted in his seat again, intensely uncomfortable. She wasn't replying. Maybe she was too disgusted. Maybe she was so angry she was waiting to meet him in person before she slapped him.

Maybe she was as turned on as he was.

His laptop dinged.

Thanks, Jonny. Talk to you soon.

Jonny jumped up and paced the hotel room. He couldn't walk quite as he normally did because his hard-on was becoming distinctly bothersome.

Thanks? What did that mean? Thanks, but no thanks? Thanks for showing me what you're really like, you lech? Thanks for giving me evidence I can take to the police?

Thanks for the fantasy, you hot stud, it was exactly what I was thinking myself, and I'll be ripping my clothes off as soon as we get to that wall?

Jonny had always liked the internet and the freedom it gave you to meet new people, discover things, and make contact in a way that had never been possible before.

Now, he could see its downside. What was the point of a mode of communication that didn't allow you to see the person you were talking to? That relied on words rather than tone of voice, electronic representations rather than bodies?

He checked his watch. Half an hour, and he'd know what Jane meant by 'Thanks'.

CHAPTER THREE

Jane asked the cab to stop at the end of the street so she could walk to the restaurant and cool down a little bit.

As she walked Jane plucked at the neckline of her dress, lower than she was used to. She'd bought it for a Pearce Grey cocktail party a year ago, and never worn it because at the last minute she'd decided that a suit would be more professional. But tonight she'd dug it out, on Jonny's advice.

Jonny's advice. Her stomach spiralled as she thought about following it. Imagine grabbing Jay and pulling him into a cab, with the full intention of having frantic sex with him as soon as they got to her flat. This beautiful, perfect man.

Her legs swished against each other as she walked in her high heels, arousing her even more. Meeting Jay this afternoon, and then Jonny's unexpected words on the laptop, had conjured up images in her head that were almost shockingly explicit. She wouldn't quite have expected it of Jonny, not something so blatantly sexy. But then again, in the past, their online relationship had been a little flirty, but mostly friendly. She'd made it clear she had a fiancé.

For all she knew, Jonathan Cole was a sex god in real life, or at least he had the imagination of one. Maybe he had a steady stream of women who were turned on by computer geniuses in glasses, and he was doing them all up against a variety of walls all over the north of England.

The thought made her smile, and it also made a twinge of jealousy tickle deep in her chest. Because Jonny's words had struck something in her, had interested her more than just anybody's sexual fantasy would've done.

It was an insight into Jonny she'd never had before…and also an insight into her own desires. Every single thing he had described had sounded exciting and perfect and right, even though she'd never done anything like that before.

And it bothered her a little bit that he might be describing his experience with someone else. Even though she fully intended to experience it with someone else, too.

Jane paused at the door of the wine bar where she'd arranged to meet Jay before dinner, and took a deep breath. It was very difficult to believe she had a date with a male model, and even more difficult to believe that she planned to seduce him, if she could.

She pushed open the door. The bar was crowded, but she spotted him immediately, as if she had been programmed to find him.

He wore a stylish dark suit and a patterned white shirt, open at the collar. His brown hair was short and casually styled. He'd shaved and without a shadow of a beard his jaw was even stronger and more defined, emphasising his cheekbones.

She bit her lip, and then remembered she would ruin her lipstick.

He checked his watch; his expression looked a little anxious, and that gave Jane a boost of confidence. He was waiting for her. When he looked around the room she stepped forward and approached the table.

Jay stood when he saw her and strode to meet her, and his smile took her breath away.

'You came,' he said, and his voice sounded almost comically relieved. He kissed her on her cheek, and she could smell the subtle scent of his shaving lotion. His lips were gentle and welcoming and they made a shiver run through her.

He stood back and looked her over, from head to foot. She'd been aroused walking in here, but under his gaze she felt her nipples hardening inside her silk bra, and felt a bolt of warmth between her legs.

'You look fantastic,' he said.

'Thank you.' With him looking at her like that, she could almost believe it. He was a charmer, she knew, but she could use all the confidence she could get, especially when in the company of a physically perfect male who was wearing a suit that fitted as if it were made for him.

'You look great,' she told him, because he really did, though she was also sure he heard that all the time.

She was a little surprised when his cheeks flushed slightly with pleasure. 'Thanks,' he said, and took her hand to lead her to the table, where he pulled out a chair for her.

He'd done that twice today, she remembered. She worked with men all the time and they rarely did anything like that. It was a totally unnecessary courtesy, a little bit of gender conditioning that she would normally laugh at, but just this minute it felt nice.

She sat in her chair and crossed her legs, letting her skirt slide up her bare thighs. She saw Jay notice, and saw him swallow.

Thank you, Jonny, she thought.

'I was worried you wouldn't show up,' he said as he sat down. 'I thought you'd decide I was coming on too strong and run in the opposite direction.'

'I'm the one who invited you out, remember?'

A waitress appeared. 'Do you fancy a glass of champagne?' Jay asked Jane. 'I feel that we've got a lot to celebrate.'

She nodded, and the waitress disappeared. 'I don't usually drink champagne,' Jay said, with a short laugh. 'Then again, I don't normally wear suits, either. One of the few perks of the modelling job is that I get to keep some of the clothes, but I don't get much call to dress up in my day-to-day life.'

'I'm not really a dress person, either,' Jane admitted.

'I'm glad you wore it, though.' His voice was quiet, intense, and Jane wanted to bite her lip and melt into a puddle. Instead, she remembered Jonny's advice and twisted a strand of her hair loosely around her finger.

He noticed, and moistened his lips with his tongue. 'Jane, that is really working,' he said. He reached his hand out as if he were about to touch her, and then the waitress came back with their drinks.

They lifted their glasses, and touched the rims together. 'Here's to seeing you,' Jay said.

'You too.' Jane took a sip of champagne, wondering if it would give her a bit more courage. 'I never thought I'd be out on a date with a male model.'

'Ah. Well, yes.' Jay put down his glass, and leaned forward on the table. 'I want to tell you about that. It's strictly temporary.'

'Really?' She suppressed dismay that he wanted to discuss business. 'Does this mean you wouldn't be available for a follow-up Giovanni Franco campaign?'

He raised his hands. 'I'm—it depends. I wouldn't leave you in the lurch, Jane. But it's not the campaign I'm talking about, it's me. I want to be honest with you and tell you why I'm modelling in the first place. It's not a career I would've ever chosen for myself.'

'Okay,' she said, wondering why he was talking about this, and leaning back in her chair with her glass of champagne.

'Okay,' he repeated after her. He took a deep breath and laid his hands on the table, gazing at them, and Jane was surprised that his expression was apprehensive, as if he were gearing himself up to say something difficult to her.

He raised his head and looked straight at her. 'I loved my dad,' he said.

Jay said the four words with such clarity and vehemence that Jane blinked. 'All right,' she said, slowly, wondering why Jay, a near stranger, was telling her this on their first date.

'He was my hero,' Jay continued. 'I thought he was everything a man should be. He seemed so honourable, so upright. He worked hard and he always had time to give me advice, and he adored my mother, I was sure he did. You could tell it by the way he looked at her, how he spoke to her. I thought he never wanted anything but to protect her.'

He met her eyes again, as if testing whether she understood what he was trying to say. Jane nodded, and, although she was still wondering why he was telling her this, his dark blue eyes were so full of sincerity and emotion that she couldn't question him too much. This was important to Jay, and for some reason it was also important to him that he told her about it.

It was unusual, but it was a kind of trust.

'I was devastated when he died. Not as much as my mother was. As she is.'

He lapsed into thought for a moment, and then shook his

head and ran his hand through his short hair. 'Anyway, she was in no state to go through his affairs, so I did it for her when I got back. And, Jane—' he rumpled his hair again, looking at Jane with pain in his features '—he'd left nothing. Everything was gone. The business, the property, all of it was mortgaged up to the hilt, and he had debts and loans adding up to thousands and thousands of pounds.'

Jane put down her drink and stared at Jay.

He was being totally sincere. Every word he said told her how hurt he was. She could tell, not only from the content of what he was saying, but also from his expression, how he spoke, the timbre of his voice. This man wasn't just worried about his parents' financial situation; he felt betrayed, disillusioned, bitterly disappointed.

'How did it happen?' she asked.

'A combination of things, though I'm not sure of all of it. Some of it was risky investment. Some of it was business losses that he borrowed more money to cover. A lot of it was gambling. Online poker, among other things. He must have been doing it in secret for years.'

She put her hand on his. 'That's awful. I'm so sorry.'

Jay nodded. 'I haven't told my mother. I couldn't bear to destroy her image of him. And I know he didn't mean to leave her in such debt; he'd had heart problems but his death was sudden. But I've had to do some scrambling to buy some time to repay the loans, and I need to do everything I possibly can to make money. I've done some extra consultancy work, and taken on some extra projects, and then when Thom started bugging me again to do some modelling for him, I said yes, even though it was something I never really wanted to do.'

'So you're modelling just to pay your father's debts.'

'Yes.' He let out a long breath, and smiled at her. Not the million-watt model smile, but a dimmer, sadder one. 'It feels good to tell you about it. Thom doesn't know. Nobody knows. My mother thinks I've suddenly developed a love of having my photograph taken.'

She squeezed his hand. 'I know what it's like to keep a secret,' she said. 'It shouldn't be hard, because all you have to do is keep your mouth shut and act normal. But it is.'

She thought about the past few days at work, seeing Gary, knowing what had happened between them, and pretending that everything was all right.

'It feels better once you've told somebody,' she said, remembering the relief she'd felt typing her problems to Jonny.

He turned his hand over so he was clasping hers. 'It feels better now I've told *you*.'

Why me? she was about to ask, and then she looked from their clasped hands to his face. There was warmth in his eyes, gentleness and earnestness in his mouth, and every line was familiar in that unexpected way.

This intimacy had been between them since they'd first seen each other, and although Jane couldn't explain it, she couldn't deny it, either.

Instead she bit her lip and nodded.

'You're so beautiful, Jane,' Jay murmured, his dark blue eyes still looking into hers. The air around them thickened, time seemed to slow even though her pulse sped up. He was so close, she was sharing every breath he took.

Jonny's words swam into her mind. He'd described this moment. And then he'd described what could happen afterwards.

She could have her mouth on this man's mouth, his hands on her, lifting her up so she could wrap her legs around his waist, pushing her clothing aside so he could enter her. Fast and hard and breathless.

The idea, the imagined feeling, throbbed inside her.

She didn't know Jay. And she didn't know if the way he made her feel was just part of his natural charm, a normal reaction of every female to his looks and his behaviour.

But she did know she wanted him. And he appeared to want her, too.

She had been engaged for eight months and had never felt even remotely this turned on. And after the hell of the past few days, after the habit and hard work of the past few years, this seemed too miraculous not to seize with both hands.

Jane lifted her free hand to Jay's face. She touched his left cheekbone and ran her fingertips down over his skin, over the place where his smile dug grooves in his cheek, close to the side of his mouth. His skin was smooth and almost shockingly warm. He tilted his head slightly, as if to press her fingers closer.

'I don't think I want dinner,' she said, and heard that her voice had become husky.

'Me neither.'

They stood at the same time, their hands still clasped. Jay dropped a note on the table and they walked out of the bar together, saying nothing. Jane was aware of every part of her body: the way her high heels made her hips sway, the brushing of her bare thighs together under her dress, the soft material of her skirt against her legs, the way her breasts moved slightly as she walked. Her fingers, twined with Jay's, which were long and strong and sinewy.

She was aware of his body, too. He moved easily but she sensed urgency in his movements. He held her hand tight and kept her close so that her shoulder and hip grazed against him two or three times as they threaded through the tables. She could even sense his breathing, rapid and shallow.

He was about six inches taller than she was, even while she was wearing heels. She would have to stand on her tiptoes to kiss him.

Jay pushed open the bar door and as soon as they were outside on the pavement Jane tugged him to one side, turned, and grabbed the lapel of his suit with her free hand to pull him towards her.

'Great idea,' he murmured, and she felt his strong arm curl around her waist and hold her close against him while she was standing up on her tiptoes, reaching with her mouth for his.

It was like no other kiss she had ever had in her life. His lips were warm and fitted against her mouth perfectly and they felt so new, strange and right. For a moment their mouths just pressed together and Jane felt as if she had taken a giant leap forward into a whole different world.

And then it was hunger. Jane tore her hands from his grip and his suit and grasped his head with both hands, burying her fingers in his soft, short hair and pulling him closer. Her mouth moved with his and the kiss changed from static to frantic. He nudged her lips open and she touched the hot, slippery tip of his tongue. She heard herself groan in her throat and that seemed to urge Jay on because he pulled her tighter and kissed her harder.

She slid her hands down his neck and gripped his broad shoulders. Somewhere in the back of her mind she remembered Jonny's description of kissing on the pavement, touching every bit of flesh that was possible, and she slipped the fingers of one hand between the buttons of his shirt. His chest was smooth and firm and his heartbeat hammered under his ribs and muscle.

It wasn't enough. With her other hand she pulled at his shirt at the back under his jacket. She tugged it out of his suit waistband and spread her hand against the small of his back, moulding it to his muscle and feeling the strength of his spine.

'Jane,' Jay muttered roughly into her mouth, closing his teeth gently on her top lip and then kissing it before he dipped his head to kiss her neck. He still held her up against him with one arm, but the other hand stroked up her back and came round to rest on her throat and collar-bone. The tips of his fingers just edged beneath the neckline of her dress and she felt his chin and mouth underneath her ear, downwards onto the base of her neck. She could feel everywhere that he wasn't touching, the inches of skin between his hand and where her breast began. His tongue tasted her and she shuddered and let her head fall back to give him better access.

People were walking past, they were in the centre of Chelsea, but she didn't care, because she had never felt this free before. Jane closed her eyes and shut out London. She concentrated on this man, who knew just how to touch her and what she wanted, who seemed more full of passion than any man she had ever met.

Strength and sinew. Her body was pressed full-length against him; his leg between her thighs, his arm wrapped round her. The rigid length of his erection against her belly told her he wanted her as much as she did him.

But beneath his ardent kisses, the clasp of his hands and the rapid pace of his breathing she could sense a tenderness in his embrace. His hands were careful. His lips were gentle even when devouring her. Quite unexpectedly, she thought of the words he had used to describe how his father had treated his mother: *he adored her.*

She felt sexy, and adored.

Jane opened her eyes, suddenly desperate to look at Jay and see the expression on his face as he kissed her. She straightened her head, and blinked as she realised she was looking straight into the lens of a camera.

Click.

'Um—we're being watched,' she said, her voice unsteady. Jay stopped kissing her and straightened, still holding her tight.

The camera clicked again. It was held by a man dressed in an anorak and shorts, wearing a floppy hat and carrying an orange backpack. Jane took in the street for the first time and noticed a group of people just past them, all carrying identical backpacks and cameras.

Tourists. And it seemed that she and Jay were suddenly a major attraction.

'Excuse me, mate,' Jay said, 'but do you mind?'

The man lowered his camera. 'You don't see that in Oklahoma City,' he said, apparently by way of explanation, and walked off after the rest of his group.

Jane tilted back her head to look at Jay's face. He was watching the man retreat, incredulity in his features. He glanced down at Jane and then both of them were laughing, holding onto each other, sharing breath again.

'I'd have thought you were used to cameras by now.' Jane giggled.

'I'm a model, not a porn star,' Jay said, and then he smiled down into her face. 'You're incredible, Jane. What next?'

She tucked his shirt back in and smoothed her other hand over the wrinkles she had made in the front of it. 'I think we need to go somewhere more private,' she said. 'Let's get a cab.'

'How private?' His expression became less playful, more serious. 'It turns out I'm only staying a few streets from here, but if you'd rather go somewhere else—'

'We don't need a cab, then.' Swiftly Jane bent down and

removed her high heels. She took his hand, dangling her shoes from the other. 'Come on, let's run to your hotel.'

Jay didn't hesitate. He took off down the pavement, with Jane running beside him as fast as she could. Her bare feet slapped on the asphalt and her hair flew out behind her and she wondered, *When was the last time I ran like this?*

With Jay's hand in hers, she flew over the kerbs, ducked between pedestrians, rounded corners like a Formula One racer and heard her breath coming out in sure, rapid pants of laughter.

They were at the door of the hotel almost before she was ready and they spilled through it laughing and gasping for breath. It was a boutique hotel, newly renovated, modern and airy. Jay brought her straight to the lift.

'I assume you want to go to my room,' he said, stroking her hair back from her flushed face and combing through its tangled waves with his fingers.

She stood on her toes and whispered into his ear. 'I can think of some things we can get up to in the lift.'

He raised his eyebrows at her and seemed to be opening his mouth to say something when they were joined by a man in tweed. The door dinged and the man came into the lift with them.

Jane held Jay's hand and nestled close into his side. *Curses*, she mouthed at him while the other passenger was pressing his floor button, and she was rewarded with Jay's sexy smile.

First floor. Second floor. Jane watched the numbers on top of the lift door, felt Jay's thumb circling the inside of her wrist, and tried not to go insane with anticipation. At the third floor the doors slid open and Jay led her out into the hallway.

'Not far, I hope,' she said.

'Just here.' He removed a card key from the inside pocket of his suit jacket and opened the door. Without a single iota of hesitation Jane walked into this near-stranger's hotel room and felt as free and young as she had ten minutes before when she'd been sprinting full-tilt with him down the King's Road.

The room was high-ceilinged and painted in light colours, furnished in sleek modern pieces. She spotted a pair of jeans over a chair, a laptop on the desk, and a big, smooth bed.

Jay closed the door behind her and she faced him.

Aside from his breathing, the rustle of his suit, and her heartbeat in her ears, the room was absolutely silent. Jane realised, with a twist of her heart, that for the first time she and this man were alone together. Actually acting out the intimacy they'd adopted from the start.

Jay reached out with a hand and pushed a lock of her hair back with his finger. Then, slowly, he dropped his arm to his own side.

'So, Jane,' he said quietly, 'what do you want to do?'

CHAPTER FOUR

THIS was it. Jane's chance to say no, to go back to her normal life, back to thinking about nothing but work, back to playing it safe.

She didn't hesitate. 'I want you,' she said and stepped back into Jay's arms.

Their kiss was, if anything, more passionate, although Jane wouldn't have believed that was possible. But this time they were alone and there was an inevitability about what was going to happen that fuelled her desire. They kissed in hungry bites. Jane's hands clutched Jay's clothing, pulling his lithe, muscular body as tight as she could. He held her with one broad hand spread across the small of her back, and his erection pressed into her, even more insistent than before.

She had to break her mouth from his for a moment to catch her breath. When she did he stepped back, just a little bit, his hands still on her, and looked her up and down. His dark blue gaze felt like hands on her body.

'Jane, you are beautiful,' he said.

Silly as it was, honesty compelled her to shake her head. 'You're the beautiful one.'

He had a face that looked both sensual and intelligent, and a body made to wear clothes, tall and lean and hard. Although she was sure he would look even better out of his clothes. She licked her lips in anticipation and tasted him on them.

'You're beautiful,' he insisted. 'More than I could have imagined you. Look.'

He turned her so she could see their reflection in the full-length mirror that covered the bathroom door. Her dress was plain, but slim and black and flattering; one of the straps was slipping off her shoulder. Her brown hair looked as if she'd just got out of bed—or run a quarter of a mile. Her cheeks were flushed with desire and excitement, her eyes were smoky and heavy-lidded, and her lips were pink and slightly swollen with Jay's kisses.

She wasn't sure about beautiful, especially when she compared herself to the perfection standing beside her. But she did look wanton, impulsive, sexy. Not really herself, but someone better.

The thought made her even more determined. She caught Jay's gaze in the mirror and held it. Slowly, deliberately, watching Jay's eyes the entire time, Jane reached beneath the hem of her dress. She hooked her fingers into the waist of her G-string and slid it down her legs. Then she stepped out of it, leaving the scrap of black lace on the carpeted floor.

Jay actually growled.

In a split second he had turned her again to face him, had grabbed her and pressed her back against the wall near the entrance door and was kissing her with even more urgency than before. He stood between her legs and with one hand lifted one of her thighs so it wrapped around his hip. The pose pushed her dress upwards and she felt the soft cloth of his suit and his hard muscles rubbing against the sensitive skin of her inner thigh.

She'd been thinking about it too long, and she was desperate to touch his naked skin after the teasing sample between the buttons of his shirt. She pushed his jacket from his shoulders, and as he shrugged it off to fall behind them she tore at his shirt. Smiling a little at their impatience, Jay helped her to remove it and she dropped it, too, on the floor.

She couldn't breathe for a minute.

He was even more perfect than she'd imagined.

All lean muscle and taut, tanned skin. His chest was smooth, and a thin line of dark hair ran from his navel down under the waistband of his trousers. Jane tore her gaze away from him to look in the mirror to her right, and saw the strong line of his shoulder and back, the way his ribs made a gentle ripple down his side.

She saw herself reach out and touch him. And then she had

to look away from the mirror, back to real life, and watch her hands travel eagerly over his naked chest. His skin was hot. She rested her right palm on him and felt the point of his nipple under her hand, and his heart beating rapidly. The fingers of her other hand explored his right nipple; it was flat against his chest, but hard in the middle where it stuck out.

She wondered if his nipples were as sensitive as hers were; she rolled the tip experimentally between her finger and thumb and was rewarded by his sharp intake of breath.

'I need to touch you, Jane,' he muttered roughly and ran his hands up the inside of her thighs, pushing her dress up even further towards her hips. His fingers brushed the curls between her legs. Jane shuddered and gripped his bare shoulders. She was held up only by his body and the wall; her own legs were suddenly boneless.

Slowly, much more slowly and gently than she would have expected after the hunger in his voice and his kiss, Jay's fingers stroked her, parting her. She could feel that she was slippery against him, and she squirmed a little in embarrassment. He had to know she was turned on, but maybe not quite how turned on, how aroused she'd been all evening.

'You're so wet, darling,' he whispered, 'it's wonderful. Let me please you.'

'You're pleasing m—' she started, but then one of his fingers stroked across her clitoris, and the pleasure was so sudden and so great that she yelped.

She saw Jay smile at that, wide and dazzling and, oh, so sexy, and then he was caressing her again, gentle circles around her clitoris, sending wave after wave of delight through her. Then his finger slid inside her, doing all sorts of wonderful things to her nerve endings.

Jane closed her eyes and let her head fall back against the wall. She'd never felt like this before. Jay's hand kept up its work, making swirls against her, pushing inside her and then coming out again to stroke her where she was most sensitive.

This man was not only beautiful, he was the best lover she had ever had in her life, and they weren't even naked yet.

Jay leaned forward and, with his free hand, pushed one strap of her dress from her shoulder. He began kissing and nibbling the slope of her naked breast, finally nudging the fabric of her dress down and taking her nipple into his mouth.

Jane cried out. Her eyes snapped open in surprise at the sound of her own voice. Jay lifted his head from her breast and looked into her face. He stilled his hand on her, cupping her sex. She was exposed to him, her legs open for him, her breast free of her dress, shiny with moisture from his mouth, reflected by the mirror beside them.

Suddenly the full impact of what she was doing slammed into her. She was in a hotel room with a stranger with his hands and mouth all over her, and how many women had he done this with?

And then he smiled at her, digging those creases in his cheeks, making his eyes sparkle. A big grin, a wonderful grin of complicity.

'I never thought we'd be doing this,' he said to her.

'It wasn't exactly in my diary for the week,' she replied, and her voice was breathless and shaking. But she couldn't help smiling back at him.

He kissed her cheek. 'It's an adventure, Jane. Will you trust me?'

She felt herself throbbing against his fingers, every fibre of her body clamouring for release.

She nodded.

His grin widened, and she could have sworn that it had turned just a little bit devilish. 'I know this wasn't part of the plan. But I really want to.'

What plan? she opened her mouth to ask, but suddenly he was kneeling before her, and his head was between her legs, and his mouth was on her.

Jane gasped in surprise. Then Jay moved his lips and tongue and she was lost. His gentleness was gone; he licked at her urgently, hot liquid strokes that sent ecstasy flowing through her.

She tangled the fingers of both hands in his short hair and brought him even closer, needing more, needing everything.

It can't get any better than this, she thought, her head spinning, her entire body focused on Jay and his mouth, so when her orgasm came it astonished her even more.

One moment she was leaning back on the wall, drowning in sensation, feeling Jay's soft hair and his hot mouth; the next she was bracing herself with both hands on the wall, her hips bucking, her head tossing from side to side, every muscle convulsing and her head ringing with the sound of her own cries.

When she could breathe again he had stood and was looking at her with his blue eyes. His smile was no longer devilish; instead he looked as if he were full of wonder.

'I love the way you give yourself to how you feel,' he said to her and kissed her. She could taste herself on his lips, unbelievably arousing.

'I want you now,' she gasped. Her hands moved, without her needing to think of it, to his trousers. She unbuckled his belt with shaking fingers and he pushed down his trousers, his boxers, every movement now frantic with need.

Jane let her fingers curl around his erection. He was hot and hard and big against her palm. She heard him groan loudly in her ear.

'This is much better than my fantasy,' he said, pressing a kiss and another onto the side of her face. 'Let me get some protection, darling.'

He stooped swiftly and pulled a packet out of his trousers. Jane, breathing heavily, quirked up the side of her mouth in a wry smile.

'Expecting this to happen?'

'I must admit I was hoping it would.' She watched him take the condom out of its wrapper and roll it down over his length. He was perfect. Every inch of him. And she wanted to possess him so badly.

She reached out to him and he stepped back into her arms and kissed her. She expected it to be wild but it wasn't, it was tender. But her breast pressed against his bare chest, and she could feel the weight of his erection on her belly, and she couldn't help but wrap her leg around him, arch her hips and pull him towards her.

He made a soft moan of pleasure against her lips and then he pulled his mouth a fraction from hers. 'Jane,' he said, his voice low and husky with desire, 'before we do this, you need to be sure that it's right. We can stop now, if you want to.'

'I don't want to stop,' she said, and kissed him, hard.

He might do this all the time. He probably could if he wanted to. He was certainly good at it. But she didn't care because right now he was with her, nobody else, and she felt more desirable and full of desire than she ever had in her life.

Jay moaned again, and lifted her with his strong hands on her hips. By instinct, she wrapped her legs around his waist and before she could even draw a breath he thrust deep inside her.

'Ah, Jane, you feel amazing,' he whispered and began to move in and out of her, building the ecstasy all over again.

Jane curved her arms around his neck and held on tight, barely able to breathe, barely able to believe this incredible thing was happening to her, to her and him together. In the mirror beside them she could see his body, lean and strong, his skin dark against her white legs and her dress. She saw his muscles clench with every push into her. The skin of his buttocks was paler where his tan ended; somehow it made him look less purely godlike, more human.

Jane turned her face back to him and saw how pleasure had softened his features, dilated his blue eyes. She caught his breath in her mouth and kissed him.

Another orgasm began to tremble inside her. She rocked her hips against Jay and let the sensation possess her again. She felt herself squeezing him inside, contracting around him, and with a final, urgent, shuddering thrust he exploded within her.

'Jane,' he murmured, still holding her tight. 'Oh, Jane. Oh, wow.' He kissed her mouth, her cheek, her forehead. She felt their hearts pounding together. Underneath her hands his neck and shoulders were damp with sweat. For a couple of minutes they both just breathed.

A little bit of sense began to swim its way into her bliss-clouded mind. She had to be heavy. But Jay just held her to him, pressing soft kisses onto her face, as if he were never going to let her go.

He was strong and he held her steady and little aftershocks of satisfaction coursed through her body. But her good sense was growing. And now that her brain had got rid of the massive amounts of hormones pumping through it she remembered that she, Jane Miller, did not do things like this. She was not a wild sexual creature. She was…quite a bit less than that.

And up until five days ago, she'd been engaged to another man.

She shifted a little bit in Jay's embrace and he gently set her down on the floor. He kissed her once more before she felt him slipping out of her, and he stepped back to take care of the condom.

And who was he, anyway? He was beautiful, and she liked him. Jane pulled up the strap of her dress and watched as a slight wry grimace crossed his face as he removed the condom.

Scratch that, she liked him a lot.

But she worked with him. In fact, he worked for her; she was his employer. And what they'd done was way, way beyond the professional.

He tossed the condom into a nearby bin and then looked back at her with that warm, humorous grin.

'That was the best idea I have ever had,' he said.

He looked quite ridiculously happy, even with his trousers and underwear still pooled around his shoe-clad feet, and Jane swallowed. She really did like him a lot. But that didn't mean that this had been a good idea, at all.

Her career was all she had left, and she'd jeopardised it, yet again, by mixing it up with her love life.

She bit her lip, and ran her hands through her untidy hair.

Jay was kicking off his shoes, and then he pulled up his boxers and trousers. The sex-saturated part of her was sorry to lose the sight of his naked lower half, but the sensible part of her was relieved, because she didn't need any more temptation tonight.

'So what would you like to do now?' he asked her cheerfully. 'Shall we go find something to eat, or would you like to explore the rest of that fant—?'

He stopped abruptly when he met her gaze, and she saw his expression transform from happiness to concern. He closed the small distance between them.

'Jane? Are you all right?'

She cleared her throat, because she wanted her voice to be

steady when she told him she was going to have to leave. 'I'm fine. But, Jay—'

He frowned. 'Don't call me that, sweetheart. Not while we're alone.'

Jane frowned back at him. 'What do you want me to call you?'

'By my real name.' He tilted his head in that way he had and gave her a half-smile, straightening the strap of her dress.

'What's your real name?'

He looked as if he was about to laugh, and then he apparently read the confusion on her face, because he stopped and shook his head. 'You're funny, Jane, but it's not a game now.'

Something was wrong. Her stomach sank, felt cold. Jane stepped around him, away from the wall, so she wasn't so close. 'What do you mean, a game? This wasn't a game.'

Jay's beautiful face was just about the most expressive thing she'd ever seen. The look on it now made her feel even colder; it was dawning dismay.

'Oh, my God,' he said.

'What's going on, Jay?' she asked, crossing her arms in front of her chest. As if that could erase what they'd just done.

'You don't know who I am, do you?'

'You're Jay Richard, the model we hired for the Franco cologne campaign. Except you said that's not your real name.'

Had he been deceiving her, somehow? Playing with her? Anger began to filter in, nearly as strong as her mounting panic. 'Have you lied to me?'

'I—' Jay ran his hands through his hair. 'Jane, I'm Jonny.'

'You're—'

She felt her legs wobble underneath her and she grabbed at the bathroom door handle, the nearest solid object. Jay—no, wait, Jonny—put his hand out to steady her, but she backed away from him.

'Jonny?' she gasped. 'Jonathan Cole? My Jonny?'

'Yeah. I—I thought you knew.'

She couldn't quite breathe. She shook her head. He was staring at her, wide-eyed, and she thought she was probably doing exactly the same thing to him.

Her thoughts whirled around her brain at about a million miles a minute and she had no idea what to say so she said the first thing that occurred to her.

'Where are your glasses?'

'On the desk, near the laptop. I'm wearing contacts.' His voice also sounded stunned.

Automatically, she looked over at the desk, seeing again his laptop open on it. His laptop where he'd told her exactly what to do on their date together.

She looked back at Jonny. Jane could see a definite emotion beginning to dawn on his face, beyond surprise.

Guilt.

Her own emotions came into sharp focus.

'You gave me *instructions* on what to do on our date?' she cried.

Jonny held up his hands. 'I didn't mean—'

'You didn't mean to? You mean you told me how to have sex with you by mistake?'

She didn't feel wobbly any more; she felt furious. She stepped forward from the wall and Jonny stepped back.

'You did ask me first,' he pointed out. He still looked guilty.

'I asked you what you would like on a hypothetical date of your own, not on an actual date with me!'

'Jane—' He reached towards her again, but then seemed to think better of it. 'You enjoyed it, though, didn't you?'

Enjoyed it? She still was feeling aftershocks of pleasure. Her body wanted to leap on him again and see what they could do up against another wall.

'That's not the point,' she said instead. 'The point is that you didn't tell me who you were and then you—' She looked down at herself. 'You even told me what to wear.' Her pulse was racing with anger, but she felt her cheeks begin to flush, too. With humiliation.

'I did tell you who I was. I sent you an email.'

'I didn't get it.'

He frowned. 'It must have gone missing. Didn't you—?'

'In any case, you didn't try all that hard to identify yourself. You let me call you Jay.'

'Yes, when we were with other people. I told you, I don't want people to know who I really am.'

'Including me,' she said bitterly. She tried to remember whether she'd called him Jay when they were alone. She wasn't certain, but she must have done, at least once? In the throes of passion, perhaps? Her face got hotter.

'I thought you knew who I was,' he said. 'You acted as if you recognised me, when you first saw me.'

'I'd seen your photographs.'

'And you didn't recognise me from them, either? Jane, we've known each other for years.'

'You—' *You used to be a geek, and now you're perfect.* She couldn't say that. 'You weren't wearing your glasses.'

'You didn't recognise me because I wasn't wearing glasses?' He sounded incredulous. 'It is Clark Kent in reverse,' he muttered.

'We were eleven the last time we saw each other,' Jane defended herself. 'A lot has changed.'

'Not that much,' Jonny said, and this time his voice was sad. 'I recognised you right away.'

Jane couldn't help but think of what she'd looked like the last time she'd seen Jonny. She'd been a tomboy, with tangled hair and probably a dirty T-shirt and skinned knees.

And apparently she hadn't changed at all.

She'd thought she couldn't get any more humiliated, but it crept further along her spine, made her want to double over and cover her head with her arms and run away.

'I trusted you,' she said, and her voice wobbled. Tears burned dangerously close to the surface.

She'd trusted him, both as Jonny and Jay, and now they both knew that she was so hopeless at being a desirable woman that she had to get instructions from the man she was dating on how to be sexy.

'Jane—' Jonny reached for her again with his strong arms. She could see softness, maybe pity, in his eyes. He wanted to hug her, to comfort her, and this was her friend and now her lover, and she'd exposed more of herself to him than she'd shown to anyone in a very long time.

If she cried in front of him that would be the final helpless step in her destruction.

She stepped quickly to one side and pulled open the hotel-room door. Anger was strong, and anger would save her.

'I never want to see you again,' she said, and wheeled out of the door.

CHAPTER FIVE

JANE turned her chair so it was facing away from the full-length windows looking out into the rest of the office, and massaged her aching cheeks. Fake smiles must use more muscles than real ones, and she'd been at it all day.

Somebody knocked on her door. Instantly Jane whirled around in her chair, her expression composed and friendly. 'Come in.'

Amy, her art director, entered. She was small and cute and, currently, the only other woman working in the creative team at Pearce Grey. In usual circumstances, Jane supposed this would bond them together. She'd expected them to bond together when Amy had been hired. She wasn't quite sure why they hadn't.

'I'm not interrupting anything, am I?' Amy asked, poking her head inside. The query was pure politeness; the entire office could see, if they wanted to, that Jane wasn't deep in work.

'Not at all, please come in.'

Amy entered and perched on the armchair across from Jane's desk. Her dark brown fringe flopped in her eyes until she flicked it aside. 'Well, I have to thank you,' she said.

Jane smiled. This time, for real. 'Why?'

'Because I love photo shoots. I love them. The clothes and the noise and those hot lights.' She gave a little shudder of pleasure. 'And the models. Thank you for asking me to go, Jane.'

'How is it going?'

It was purely a professional question, of course. Jane was in charge of the Giovanni Franco campaign and therefore she needed to be up to speed on every aspect of its production. It wasn't a question about Jonny at all. In fact, she'd been too busy to think about Jonny all day.

Except for every five minutes or so when she was broadsided by a sensual memory of them tearing at each other's clothes. Or a sickening memory of herself, typing her heart out onto her laptop.

'Great! Absolutely perfect.' Amy sighed happily. 'We made completely the right decision choosing Jay Richard as a model. The guy is a natural for Franco cologne. He's got that relaxed attitude, you know?'

'He was relaxed?' Yes. It made sense that Jonny would be relaxed, even after what had happened last night. He'd probably had a hearty post-coital dinner and then tumbled into a restful post-coital sleep.

'He's got a talent in front of the camera. And he's such a nice bloke! Not at all up himself. Very friendly.'

Yes, you should see how friendly he likes to get with his friends. Jane did her best to look interested.

'And delectable, of course. He had his shirt off at one point. My God.' Amy pretended to fan herself.

'Are you looking for a boyfriend?' Jane asked, a little too quickly.

Amy laughed. 'As if a model would be interested in a twenty-seven-year-old single mum. No, I was just window-shopping.' She evidently caught Jane's expression and her smile faded. 'Is something wrong?'

'No.' Jane rubbed her forehead and gave Amy another smile, this one rueful. 'I've been working too hard, I guess.'

'Well, you've got a lot on. I was thinking about creative director some day, you know, but, watching you, I don't think I could cope with the workload. I work hard, but you're amazing.'

'Just dedicated.'

Not quite dedicated enough, though, apparently. Checking up on how the photo shoot was going should have been Jane's job; it was the sort of thing she prided herself on doing, the little extra bit of personal care for Pearce Grey's clients. But this morning, the thought of going to see Jonny posing in front of a camera had been too much to bear.

'Well, thank you for asking me to go this morning. Apparently

Thom Erikson is throwing a party on Friday and is inviting the whole office. Did you know about that?'

'Yes.' She'd found out at lunch yesterday and forgotten to send out a memo when she got back to work, because she'd been too preoccupied with her upcoming date. Just another ball she'd dropped. 'I don't think I can go. Work,' she added.

'Too bad. I hear his parties are legendary. And Thom's cute, even more hunky than his models. I'm definitely getting a baby-sitter for that night. I wouldn't miss it for the world. Though I doubt Thom Erikson would be interested in a single mum, either.' Amy perked up. 'The model asked after you, by the way.'

Jane had thought she was sitting up straight, but at that she became even straighter. 'What did he say?'

'He wanted to know why you hadn't come yourself. I told him how busy you were.' Amy played with the hem of her jumper for a minute, and then met Jane's eyes. 'Jane, are you all right?'

'I'm fine,' Jane said automatically, then thought twice. Amy wasn't Gary; she appeared to have no alternative agenda for asking how she was. 'Why do you ask?'

'Well, you know, I haven't worked here long, but you're always so busy, and then it's not like you not to go to the shoot yourself. And you seem pretty preoccupied, even considering how important this campaign is. And then even Jay asked if you were all right, and I figure if someone who barely knows you is concerned about you, then…' She trailed off. 'Well, anyway, I wondered.'

Amy's green eyes were full of kindness, and for a moment Jane was tempted to confide in her. She remembered what a relief it had felt yesterday when she'd typed Jonny the truth about her break-up. And how, when he'd told her about his father, it had seemed as if a burden was being lifted from him.

But then, of course, Jonny was evidently a very good actor. And maybe he'd felt as if he owed her a confidence in return for her blatantly showing him her insecurities. Some people worked like that, as if secrets and vulnerability were commodities.

'I'm fine,' Jane said, and in her head she heard Jonny's voice saying, *I know you've got a better vocabulary than that, even when you're lying.*

'I'm splendid, actually.' She stood up and gave Amy her widest smile.

She genuinely liked Amy, so it only hurt a little.

The glimmer of relief she had when she turned her key in the lock of her flat, home at last, died away as soon as she actually opened her door.

The place was so empty. And the hours ahead of her, even though she'd worked late, even more empty.

Habit sent her straight across the hardwood floor to her desk in the corner of the living room. She toed off her shoes, giving an involuntary sigh of blessed freedom for her feet, and pressed her laptop's 'on' button.

It hadn't finished booting up yet when she realised she'd autopiloted herself straight to the worst place in the room.

For the past few months, even when Gary had been around, this had been her favourite seat in the house. Her computer hadn't been a piece of machinery; it had been a direct line to somebody else, someone who cared. She would come home from work and look straight away for a message from Jonny. Something warm and human, even though it was through a machine.

Quite often, Jonny was online in the evening at the same time she was; he worked all hours on his computer stuff. She'd pour herself a glass of wine and chat with him, about nothing, and laugh.

Jane stared at the screen, now blossoming into colour and icons.

It was a computer. It wasn't a magic portal to her friend. It was plastic, wires, microchips, a screen that had made her feel safe enough to reveal herself.

Her chat program launched itself, and she saw that Jonny was online. She immediately shut the program down, before he could hail her.

Her inbox popped up too and she watched the numbers of unread messages mount up. There were two from Jonny. She noticed his return address without wanting to. Swiftly, she turned the computer off before she could even read the topic lines of his emails. She didn't care what he wanted to say to her.

Because the screen went blank she didn't realise right away that she was crying.

He had been one of the few comfortable things left in her life. And now he was gone.

Briefly, she buried her face in her hands. Her skull felt fragile underneath her skin, and her tears were hot.

Somebody knocked on the door.

Jane jumped out of her chair. Jonny knew where she lived, didn't he? Had he been online on a mobile device, hoping to talk with her as he travelled to her flat?

Surely he wouldn't turn up, not after what she'd said and what had happened between them. But he'd called her at work both this morning and this afternoon; she'd pretended to be too busy to take his calls.

Her stomach fluttered and she wasn't sure whether it was dread or anticipation.

She crossed to the door and looked out of the peephole. Only when she saw Gary's face did she remember that he'd asked her if he could come round to pick up a few things.

This feeling wasn't ambivalent; it was disappointment, pure and simple.

'Just a second,' she called through the door, because if she didn't answer he'd most likely let himself in with his own set of keys. The knock had been courtesy, like his asking permission to come round; in reality, Gary still owned half of this flat, at least until she bought his share from him.

She hurried to the kitchen, splashed her face with cold water and wiped it on a tea towel. She'd promised herself that Gary would never see her crying again. Even if, this time, it had nothing to do with him.

Freshening up done, she opened the door, hoping she'd eliminated all traces of her tears. Her skin was always pale, she knew, and tended to show pinkness around her eyes and nose.

'Gary,' she said, not exactly in greeting, and stepped aside to let him in.

It was odd, but even in this flat, which they'd shared for two years, Gary looked like a stranger. He stood in the room, clearing his throat and fiddling with his shirt cuffs. She wondered if she had ever found those mannerisms endearing; she couldn't remember. In fact, she couldn't remember looking at him closely at all.

'Kathleen said she ran into you,' he said.

'Yes,' Jane replied. 'Tell me, Gary, what attracted you most to her—her breasts, her cheap shoes, or her ability to balance heavy trays of food?'

Gary rolled his eyes. That trait wasn't endearing, either. 'Jane, that comment isn't worthy of you.'

Jane took a deep breath, and dropped the sarcasm. 'I just have a hard time understanding your motivation. You always encouraged me to go for promotion at work. It seemed important to you that I had a successful career. I'm wondering if that was never actually true, or if you've changed your mind about what you want in a woman.'

'Kathleen's easier to be with.'

'She's not threatening to you because she's successful, you mean. She has her little job and you're the resident big shot. Whereas the minute I got promoted to creative director, you couldn't leave me soon enough.'

'Jane, I encouraged you in your career because that's all you ever seemed to want.'

'And as soon as I got what I wanted, you got scared because you couldn't stand to live with someone who had the same status and earning power as you.'

His face was getting red.

'Kathleen is a real woman,' he shot back. 'She's sexy and beautiful and she's interested in me more than her job. You were never interested in me. You floated around in your own work world and you never took the time to get to know who I am. You never cared about my comfort, or my needs, or—'

She's sexy and beautiful…like a real woman. Despair and doubt grabbed hold of Jane's guts and anger seemed like the safest route.

'I get it now,' Jane said. 'You were looking for someone to bring you your pipe and slippers at the end of a hard day.'

'I was looking for someone who gave a damn about anything besides herself and her career!'

'I give a damn about plenty of things,' Jane snapped.

'Like what? Like who?'

'Like my mother, and my brothers, and—'

And she stopped herself, her throat closing up.

Because she'd been about to say *and Jonny*.

Somebody knocked on the door.

Jane didn't bother to look through the peephole this time; she was too preoccupied with emotion. When she opened the door a young man was standing there with a large bouquet of lilies and roses in his hands.

'Jane Miller?' he said. 'Delivery.'

In a daze, Jane took the bouquet. Its scent immediately surrounded her. She closed the door. The bouquet was so big that she could barely hold it with her left arm as she opened the card that was attached to it.

She'd never seen Jonny's handwriting before, but she recognised it right away—just as she'd recognised him and never realised it. It was neat and upright.

Dear Jane, I'm sorry for deceiving you. I didn't mean to. I don't want to lose you. Can we start again? Jonny.

It was a day for mixed emotions. Jane was flooded with both embarrassment and a huge, hopeless longing.

How on earth could they start again? Now that they'd crossed every barrier she had?

She pictured him at the florists', writing out the card, tilting his head in that way he had. Maybe furrowing his forehead a little as he thought about what he wanted to say. Or maybe dashing off the note with practised male-model charm, thinking he only had to make a little effort and a woman like her would fall all over herself to run back into his arms.

But she could see every bit of him in her mind: his blue eyes slightly narrowed, his lean body bent over the counter, his long fingers on the pen.

She'd already learned the written word could be deceptive. What did he mean, exactly, by losing her? Or by starting again? As friends? Lovers? Email buddies?

'What are those in aid of?'

Staring at the card, she'd completely forgotten about Gary. She glanced up and saw his stranger's face.

He looked jealous.

Her reaction to that wasn't mixed at all; it was glee.

That probably wasn't worthy of her, either, but somehow she didn't care.

'Oh, they're from a man I had a date with last night,' she said breezily. She inhaled deeply from the bouquet. The scent was feminine, beautiful. The sort of thing a man would give to a desirable woman. A real woman.

'You had a date? Who with?'

The emphasis was just in the wrong place, so that the meaning was clear. Gary was wondering what kind of guy would ask out a career-obsessed woman scorned.

That ruined her glee at his jealousy, and turned it back into anger. 'He's a model,' she said, and went into the kitchen to find a vase.

'A model?' She could hear Gary behind her. 'Wait, hold on. Is he the model you've got for the Franco cologne campaign? The one you went out for lunch with yesterday?'

The jealousy was back in his voice, and it felt so good to hear it that she answered without thinking. 'Yes, and then the two of us went out for dinner. Among other things.'

She glanced up as she said the last words, and had to suppress a smile because her ex-fiancé, the guy who'd dumped her out of the blue for a waitress, was red and white in the face and looked as if he'd been pounced on by a big green-eyed monster.

'Of course that's the reason I've been preoccupied all day,' she purred, her words telling the truth but her tone putting a whole other spin on them. Gary's face got redder and whiter.

The green-eyed monster was chewing him up and spitting him out.

It didn't feel as good as she'd felt when she was with Jonny. But it felt pretty damn good, nevertheless.

'I'll go get those things I came for,' he said, sounding muffled, and left the room.

Jane put the flowers in a vase, put them on the kitchen table, and sat there gazing at their lovely petals and breathing their dizzying perfume, trying to work out whether she should be feeling triumph or dread.

Pearce Grey Advertising Agency looked as if there wasn't a comfortable chair in the place. Jonny recognised the type of business immediately; he'd done some consulting for a couple of software companies with the same aesthetic. He'd only stayed as long as it had taken to finish the job and then he'd gone back home to his own happily cluttered desk.

If he'd had to guess, before a couple of days ago, he'd have said his Jane would never feel at home in such a place. She was too spontaneous, too alive and warm to belong in a cold, minimalist office. Even when he'd first seen her he'd believed that her tailored suit and her scraped-back hair were a front, a professional mask to hide the real passionate woman underneath.

Then she'd frozen him out, completely and suddenly. No calls, no emails, never online, no response to his flowers or note. She was acting on her statement that she never wanted to see him again. And while she had a good reason because their date had unintentionally turned out to be a disaster, he hadn't thought she'd be capable of such a total shutdown. He'd thought what they shared was more genuine than that.

But after what he'd heard this morning, he couldn't help but wonder now, as he strode through Pearce Grey, whether Jane did belong to a place like this after all. All appearance, no substance.

A man in a suit gave him directions to her office. A whole side of it was plate glass, and even before he got to the door he could see her, sitting at her desk and poring over papers and photographs. She was wearing black and twisting a strand of hair around her finger.

He stopped, just for a moment, with his hand on the doorknob, and watched her.

Her surroundings were one thing. That little gesture, her hair round her finger, proved Jane was another.

He hoped.

Jonny opened the door and stepped in. Jane's head lifted and their eyes met.

He was glad to see her. Just her presence was enough to make his heart beat faster. He thought he saw, for a split second, an answering gladness in her face, before it froze into a wary expression.

'Don't you have a shoot now?' she asked.

They weren't the most welcoming words in the world, but at least it was a good sign that she knew what he was supposed to be doing. It implied she cared.

Then again, it was her job to care about the shoot. Not to care about him.

'Coffee break,' he told her as he closed the door behind him. 'I decided I needed to see you more than I needed caffeine.'

Since Jonny had had to flag down a taxi and take it halfway across London in traffic to get here, he thought the photographer had probably already finished his coffee and was waiting for the model to get back. It wasn't worrying Jonny much.

She stood, stiff behind her desk. 'I thought I made my feelings pretty clear the last time I saw you.'

Jonny walked up to the desk. With the furniture as a barrier between them, she stood firm where she was. He remembered how she'd fallen into his arms outside the restaurant, and then how she'd dodged him when he'd wanted to touch her, when she'd found out who he really was. She was doing her best to look impassive, but there was a tell-tale flush on her cheeks and her eyes weren't quite steady on his.

She was reacting to him, all right. He just wished he could be sure why.

'Yes, Jane,' he said. 'You made your feelings very clear indeed. You never wanted to see me again, nor, apparently, to talk to me on the phone or communicate with me online.'

'That's right,' she said, her voice cold.

Jonny put his hands on her desk and leaned forward on his arms. With Jane standing so firm, this meant that his face was inches from hers, close enough for him to smell the flowery scent of her hair. He looked straight into her grey eyes.

'So maybe you can explain to me why you're telling everyone that we're sleeping together,' he said.

CHAPTER SIX

JANE'S eyes widened with surprise. He thought he saw something else there, too.

'I'm not,' she said.

He didn't vary his stance, still close to her.

'That's funny, because it's common knowledge, apparently, and I haven't told anybody.'

'Neither have I.' Her pointed chin thrust forward in a stubborn gesture he remembered from when she was a girl arguing with her four brothers. It was a gesture she'd used even when she was wrong.

'Well, then, there are two other options,' he said. 'Either somebody hacked into one of our computers and read the chat we had the other night, or the tourist who took our photograph outside the restaurant has been circulating it among people we know.'

'I doubt that—'

'I agree. Both of those are extremely unlikely. Which means that, since I haven't told anybody, you have.'

Jane folded her arms across her chest. 'I told you, I haven't said anything about our—about what we did.' Her cheeks flushed.

She was digging in her heels, and his confrontational stance probably wasn't helping him get at the truth. He stopped leaning on the desk and instead sat on a corner of it, facing her. Still close to her, but more casual.

'I don't mind if you told people,' he told her. 'I loved making love with you and if we were in a relationship I'd shout it from the rooftops. But I can't figure out why you'd tell anybody about what happened, after you were so angry about it.'

Jane frowned. 'Who said something to you?'

'Thom came to the shoot bursting with the news.'

Bursting was an understatement. Thom had practically been shouting with excitement that Jonny had had sex with somebody, and, moreover, somebody that Thom had—supposedly—introduced him to. Jonny didn't think he'd ever heard so many 'excellent's and 'way to go's in his life.

Jonny had had to steer his agent into a quiet corner and warn him in the strongest terms not to spread the news around. Even after that, Thom had been grinning so widely and making so many broad hints that Jonny was sure the photographer, the assistant, the make-up and hair woman, the stylist, the lighting guy, and all the other random people who seemed to hang out at photo shoots for no reason whatsoever knew that he'd got involved with the creative director of Pearce Grey.

'He said he'd had a phone call from someone here at the agency,' Jonny added. 'And I'm sorry if I've been jumping to conclusions, but it seems logical that the information came from you.'

'Stated just like a good logical software developer,' Jane said, but her flushed cheeks had gone pale, and he could definitely see now that she was looking sheepish.

'Who'd you talk to?' he asked gently.

'Gary,' she said, and she sank into her chair with a sigh.

'Your ex?'

'I didn't tell him that we'd slept together. Not in so many words. But I might have hinted a little.' She rubbed her forehead. 'I really didn't think he'd talk to anybody else.'

Jane had told her former fiancé about them? Maybe it was wrong, but the fact sent a burst of hope through Jonny. She wouldn't tell Gary about her love life unless she was serious about it and saw it going somewhere, right?

He wanted to take her hand, which was lying on the desk in front of him, but he restrained himself until he knew better what she was thinking.

'Why did you tell Gary?'

'Because I—' She pushed the stray curls of hair back from her face. 'I know I shouldn't have. But he was lording his new relationship with Kathleen over me, making me feel about two inches high. And then your bouquet showed up. So I just told him.'

Jonny looked at her face, the rueful expression. He wasn't sure he liked where this was going. 'You told him to make him jealous?'

'Well, yeah. I mean, he's going out with a waitress. And you're a—'

He definitely didn't like where this was going. He stood up, feeling anger flushing his own skin. 'You told him because I'm a model?'

'I told him because you sent a bunch of flowers to me after I'd told you I didn't want to see you again,' Jane shot back.

'And did you tell him that you didn't want to see me again?'

She bit her lip. 'I didn't get to that part.'

It was turn for Jonny to cross his arms over his chest. 'Let me get this straight. You told him that we were having an affair, to pay him back, because sleeping with a model gets more points than sleeping with a waitress?'

'This really isn't any of your business,' Jane said, doing that chin thing again. 'It's between me and Gary.'

'I'd say it was completely my business when Gary goes on to spread a rumour that you and I are having a relationship. An untrue rumour, now that you've frozen me out.' He found that he was pacing the floor in front of her desk, and stopped and looked her right in the eye. 'Jane, I hate deception. I *hate* it.'

'That should have occurred to you when you were deceiving me about who you are.'

He threw his hands up in the air. 'I told you, I sent you an email telling you about the whole thing. Haven't you read it yet, or have you been too busy trying to think of ways to get your fiancé's goat?'

'I haven't seen it.'

Her stubborn refusal to admit this basic, factual point drove him even crazier.

'So let me get something straight,' he said, 'because I didn't quite get the full truth the other night. Did you have sex with me just because of the way I looked? Not because we knew each other or had feelings about each other?'

'I—'

She didn't need to answer; he could see the truth in her eyes. She looked guilty as sin underneath her defensiveness.

'And you were asking me for my sexual fantasy so you could apply it to a guy who you thought was a total stranger to you? Which means, essentially, you were cheating on me with *me*?'

'You didn't exactly get the worst end of the bargain,' Jane said. 'And besides, I wasn't cheating on you; we weren't having a relationship.'

'Jane, I'm not a player. I wouldn't share these intimate details about my desires with you if I didn't have any feelings about you. I thought you knew me better than that.'

'I'm beginning to realise I don't know you at all.'

'No. Instead you judge me on my appearance. And then use my job—a job I told you I don't even like—to score points off your boyfriend.' He ran his hands through his hair. 'You're just the same as everybody else.'

The words echoed around inside him as if he were suddenly a hollow, painful space.

'Jonny, shh.'

He hadn't been looking at her; he'd been staring at blank air, overcome by yet more disillusion. He realised now that Jane had a finger to her lips and was making trying-to-be-subtle gestures with the other hand at the plate-glass office wall. Through which at least four people were staring, watching the two of them argue.

'Let them look,' said Jonny, but when he glanced back at Jane, her skin was white to the lips.

'You really care that much about what your colleagues think of you?' he said, more gently this time.

'My job is all I have left, Jonny,' she whispered, and her voice was so small and so vulnerable despite the stubbornness she'd just shown him that he felt a fierce surge of protectiveness, even through his anger.

'I didn't think Gary would tell anyone,' she continued, 'but now that he has it must be all over the agency. I hadn't even told people we'd broken up. And now they must think I—'

'Let's give them something to really think about,' said Jonny, and before he could think better of it he was on her side of the desk and was doing what he'd wanted to do since he'd walked in the door, which was taking her in his arms and kissing her.

He might be disappointed with the way Jane perceived him, but her kiss was another thing. Her lips were just as soft and warm and receptive as he remembered, that cupid's bow mouth parting underneath his to let him taste her sweetness.

In his arms, she was the girl of his dreams.

She hesitated for a split second, and then she curled her arms around his neck. He felt one of her hands thread through the hair on the back of his head and felt her body curve towards his.

Jonny wanted her even more than he had the other night. He wanted to remove every single stitch of her clothing and continue from where they'd left off. He wanted to look in her face and laugh with her as they gave each other pleasure and then afterwards hold her and talk.

He wanted to do all of that even though, down deep, he knew he was still angry with her.

For right now, he kissed her. He held her delicate face in one hand and with the other he spanned the curve of her waist. His tongue touched hers, and, though this kiss was gentler, it was fuelled by the memory of them together, desperate and hungry, kissing as if their lives depended on it as they made love.

Jane made a sound in her throat that was part pleasure, part protest. He held the kiss for another moment, because he didn't want to stop, but also because he wanted to show her he, too, had some control in this situation. Then he parted from her, still holding her, his lips only inches from hers.

'There are people,' she whispered, though she made no movement to get away from him.

'So we'll go somewhere private.'

She stiffened slightly in his arms. 'I'm not going to have sex with you again, Jonny.'

And he was an idiot to even think that a kiss was ever going to change anything between them. 'To talk,' he said.

'You have a photo shoot now,' she said.

'I don't care about the photo shoot. We have a lot to discuss.'

This time she did draw away from him, taking a step back and smoothing down her clothing. 'I care about the photo shoot. This campaign needs to be a success. And you need the money, Jonny.'

Well, there was a point, though he'd just as soon not think about it right now.

'All right. I'll come to your flat tonight.'

'No,' she replied, too quickly. 'I'll meet you for coffee at the café across the road from your hotel at seven o'clock, when we're both done with work.'

Coffee. The implications of that were pretty clear: she didn't want to commit long enough for dinner with him, nor did she want to trust the disinhibiting effect of an after-work drink. And she definitely didn't want him anywhere near her personal life.

Even though he'd just kissed her in front of everyone she worked with, and she'd made it public that they'd slept together.

'Seven o'clock,' he said, nodding curtly, and left her office.

He ignored the interested looks he gathered on his way out of the building.

Jane's insides were doing an imitation of a million drunken butterflies. Her hands were wet and she couldn't quite catch her breath as she walked the last few steps to the café.

It was worse than when she'd met Jonny as Jay, before their date.

She stopped before she reached the door and took a few deep breaths. This was why she had to meet Jonny, and ask him what she was going to ask him. Up until two nights ago, Jonny had been her friend, her safe man, her comfortable buddy.

She had to stop feeling this way about talking with him, because the alternative was too awful to bear.

She bit her lip, and the feeling reminded her of his mouth on hers this afternoon. So unexpected and so exciting. And so annoyingly perfect that even now the butterflies spun around her stomach in a tipsy little aroused dance before they settled down to their more serious business of making her feel sick.

Jane pushed open the door and saw that, just as the last time she'd arranged to meet him, Jonny was early and waiting for her.

He was wearing jeans and a red T-shirt and stylish black-rimmed glasses. He'd washed his hair and now it was free of the products that had mussed it into trendy disarray this afternoon.

Their eyes met as soon as she walked in. He stood up.

Her belly butterflies swooned and melted into a big, sticky, lustful puddle.

And she should just *get over* these feelings because they were doing no good at all. Jane brushed her clothes down unnecessarily and went to meet Jonny at his table.

'Hi,' he said. For a moment she thought he was going to make a move to kiss her—on the lips or on the cheek, she couldn't tell—but then he seemed to think better of it. 'Skinny latte with chocolate on top?'

Jane nodded and sat while he went up to the counter to get her a coffee. She couldn't remember when she'd told him how she liked her coffee, but she wasn't surprised he knew. It must have come up during one of their casual, fun exchanges of emails or chats online. She knew he liked black filter coffee, from his years in the States working as a software developer. It was part of the tonnes of information they knew about each other—information that was inconsequential, but intimate and friendly.

Unfortunately, what he looked like had never been part of their late-night chats.

She couldn't resist glancing up at the front of the café where he stood ordering her coffee. The female barista was smiling at him very widely, and two women in the queue behind him and another at a table in the corner were ogling him openly behind his back. To say nothing of the guy with the earring bussing tables, who fumbled a latte glass because he couldn't seem to take his eyes off Jonny's backside.

How did you drop that fact into casual conversation? 'Oh, by the way, Jane, I'm gorgeous and all women and even some men want me'?

Jonny came back with her coffee and a plate of biscuits. 'Lattes always remind me of the coffee my mum used to give us when we were kids,' he said. 'Remember, a spoonful of coffee and all the rest milk? She called it cowboy coffee.'

She'd forgotten about that until now. 'She put cocoa on top, too.'

'Your latte must be a comfort thing,' Jonny said, and sat across from her, taking a drink of his mug of black coffee.

And she'd never thought about that, either, though it could well be true. She was certainly in need of comfort at the moment.

'If we'd started our conversation like this the other night, we wouldn't be in all this trouble now,' she said.

'True. But then again the other night wasn't about reminiscing.'

'No,' Jane said, and she couldn't say much more than that, because the sight of Jonny's hands and mouth on his coffee mug brought inevitable reminiscences of his hands and his mouth on her.

'Did you find my email telling you who I was?' he asked quietly.

'Yes.' It had been buried in her inbox from a couple of days ago, along with all the other emails she hadn't had time or energy to deal with. It was a typical Jonny email, good-humoured and slightly self-deprecating, and after she'd read it she hadn't been able to stop herself from reading a few of his other recent emails, sent before he'd come down to London. Reminding her of that easy and freeing friendship they'd shared.

'I'm sorry I accused you of setting out to deceive me,' she said.

He nodded. 'I'm sorry you didn't know who I was.'

In the silence that followed, she took a deep drink of her latte. Now she could see that it was a grown-up version of cowboy coffee. It wasn't really as comforting as it should be.

She put down her cup. 'I don't want to lose your friendship, Jonny. It—' She hesitated, unused to exposing herself, but, this much, she had to. 'It means a lot to me that we're friends.'

'Me too.' He let out a deep breath, as if he'd been holding it the whole time she was drinking. 'You're the only person I've told about my father. And you're only the second person who knows about my two careers. It's important to me that I can trust you.'

'Okay.' She steeled herself, and then brought up the topic. 'So we've both got to agree that it's a bad idea for us to have sex again.'

He frowned. She should have expected that, she guessed—he had, after all, pretty much told her this afternoon that he'd liked having sex with her—but it was still a surprise to her that he would want to continue.

'No, I don't agree,' he said.

She set her chin, because she had to win this battle. 'Well, I do. And it takes two of us to do it.'

'It was your idea for us to have sex together in the first place,' he pointed out. 'You were the one who brought it up originally.'

'That was before I knew who you were.'

'Yes, but it proves that there's chemistry between us. Or do you usually have sex with a man on the first date?'

She wouldn't know, as she wasn't much of a dater. She wasn't exactly the type that men wined and dined and then tried to bed. 'No, I don't,' she said.

'Well, there you are.'

'You're trying to use that logic thing on me again. It's not going to work. I don't want to sleep with you, and that's that.'

'And now you're lying to me again,' he said, and his voice was quiet although Jane heard every word.

'I'm not.' Her heart was racing.

'Yes, you are. Your eyes give you away every time, Jane. You want to pick up where we left off the other night as much as I do.'

He reached across the table and touched her hand. Just one touch, one finger, between the two hills of her knuckles. It was enough to nearly make her moan.

Jonny leaned forward. Above the aroma of coffee and chocolate biscuits she breathed in his smell of shampoo and warm cotton. She remembered pressing her mouth to the side of his jaw, his skin smooth from shaving, and the strong bones underneath.

'Come on, Jane,' he murmured. 'Remember that I know you. Tell me the truth. You want to have sex with me.'

His glasses somehow made his eyes an even deeper blue. Jane felt that if she kept on looking in them she would fall under some sort of Jonny spell and never come out of it. She shifted her eyes away from him, as if she could find the strength to resist him somewhere in the café.

The two women who'd been standing behind Jonny in the queue were sitting a couple of tables away, giggling and glancing in their direction. The barista had paused while frothing milk, and had a faraway expression on her face as she gazed at Jonny. And the waiter had circled to the other end of the room to get a better view.

Yes, she wanted to have sex with Jonny. And so did half the people in this room.

'It's just not going to happen, okay?' She gave Jonny a hard look to show him she meant it and then took a drink of her latte in a way she hoped signified finality.

Jonny exhaled sharply and sat back in his chair. She had to give him credit—he didn't seem to notice that he was the focus of so many people's lust.

'Okay, I can accept that,' he said. 'For now. But do we have to put rules on this? Let's date each other, see where it takes us, and keep an open mind about the sex issue.' He tilted his head and a smile just touched his lips. 'I think I could have fun trying to persuade you to change your mind.'

It was the same naughty smile he'd given her before kneeling in front of her and giving her an orgasm.

Dear Lord, Jonny could persuade her into anything.

'I don't want to date you,' she said quickly.

Now he really did look frustrated. 'Why not?'

Because I didn't even love Gary and I couldn't hold onto him.

But that was too much to admit, not to the guy who half the café wanted. Not to the guy who was looking at her hard, as if he wanted to try to look straight through into her soul.

'Because I don't have any friends,' she blurted instead. Which was bad enough, but better than the real truth.

Jonny looked surprised.

'I don't have time,' she explained. 'I've had to work very hard to get where I am right now, and then there was Gary, and…' She trailed off, fully aware of how lame she sounded. 'I like lots of the people at work,' she added.

'But they're colleagues,' Jonny finished for her. 'And you want to put up a good front with them.'

'Not just that. It's complicated. And I really don't have the time.'

She thought of the hours last night, alone and empty, with nobody to talk with. Not even via the internet.

'I can't lose you as a friend, Jonny. If we date and it goes wrong we can never go back to how we were before. And I liked how we were before. It made me happy to talk with you.'

'I liked how we were before, too. But I'd also like more.'

She shook her head. 'I can't risk it. We've known each other since we were kids. And—Jonny, all I wanted last night was to talk to someone about what was going on, how confused I felt about what had happened between you and me and how awful I felt about Gary. I wanted to talk to *you* about it. And I couldn't because you were involved in it. I was so lonely.'

Her voice sounded pathetic to her own ears. But it was the truth, and probably the only way that she could salvage her friendship with Jonny was to trust him with this weakness.

He looked at her for a long time. Behind his glasses, behind his sharp gaze, she knew he was thinking, weighing up what she'd said, how she felt, how he felt, the whole situation. Jonny was clever; he'd always been clever, more than she was. He'd sent her a copy of one of his how-to computer books one time and she'd marvelled at how he could take something so incomprehensible and simplify it down so that anyone could understand it. That, as far as she was concerned, was a more difficult skill than understanding it in all its complexity in the first place.

She'd only presented him with the simplest of her motives for not dating him. If he was clever enough to see through her to her real fears…

'All right,' he said, finally. 'Just friends. For now.'

Jane didn't quite like how he said the last two words. It was as if he had some intention to make 'now' history as soon as possible.

'Promise me,' she said.

Jonny sighed. 'Jane, you can trust me.'

'Okay.' She bit her lip, because the most difficult part was coming next.

'So now that you've agreed that we're not dating,' she said, 'I need you to pretend that we are.'

CHAPTER SEVEN

JONNY had been about to take a drink of coffee. Instead he put it down.

'What?' he said.

'Just for a little while, until all this dies down. And you're going back up to the Lake District after you finish this job, right, anyway? So it's not for long at all.'

Jane was speaking too quickly; there were spots of red on both her cheeks. She was acting as if this were a normal thing to ask, but he could see that she knew that it was deeply strange.

'How long isn't particularly the issue,' he said. 'The issue is that you're asking me to do it at all.'

She didn't answer. She toyed with her glass and avoided his eyes.

'I want to date you, Jane. But instead you want me to pretend to do what I want to do for real.'

'If you want to do it for real, then pretending won't be so hard, will it?' She glanced up at him, and then back down at her glass.

She was most definitely not telling him everything about this. He felt the same anger and frustration he'd felt this afternoon come rushing back. 'Do you mind if I ask you why?'

'Everybody saw us this afternoon,' she said. 'Plus, it seems that Gary didn't stop with telling Thom about what I'd said to him. The entire company is buzzing about it. I mean, I hadn't even told anybody that Gary and I split up, and then all of a sudden I'm kissing the campaign model in my office.'

'So what? Tell them it's none of their business, and get on with it.'

'It's not that easy. Nobody's saying anything to me. It's just whispers.'

She met his eyes finally and he saw the baffled hurt there.

And he remembered that hurt. He remembered the whispers.

There had been a year or two, when he was a teenager at school, when he'd been the recipient of both of them. His tormentors had mostly been boys, and boys were usually pretty straightforward about their bullying. Their preferred method was generally to ambush him after school and kick him around a bit. But there had been whispers, too.

His anger could take a back seat for a moment.

'Jane, you can't let other people get to you. You have to fight back. It's one of the things my dad taught me; when I was getting beaten up at school he made me take up running and helped me learn boxing. When I was strong enough to confront the bullies, they stopped.'

'This is different,' Jane answered quickly. 'I'm not being bullied. It's just that—this job is important to me. I need the people at work to respect me. And from what's happened, it looks like I'm somebody who's been dumped by her boyfriend for another woman and has straight away thrown herself at the nearest male. I need to prove to them that I'm not desperate. And that…' She blushed harder. 'You know, you want me, too.'

'I do want you. But not like this.'

'I've already told you, we can't have a relationship. Our friendship is too important.'

Jonny felt like jumping up and pacing around the room. As they were in a crowded café, he restrained himself. But only just.

Jane must have seen how he felt because she leaned forward on the table, her hands clasped together in supplication.

'Please, Jonny. I don't want to look desperate, but I am. It's not just the people at work. It's Gary. He came to my office this afternoon and told me that since I'd found a new boyfriend, he'd be bringing Kathleen to Thom's agency party. If I turn up on my own—'

He was trying to stay calm, but it wasn't working. 'Ah. I see it now. It's back to Gary and using me to make him jealous.'

'It's not just about making him jealous.'

'But is about using me.'

Her pleading hands clasped into fists. 'Jonny, I'm asking for your help, that's all. You were the one who had to go and kiss me this afternoon! If you hadn't done that, this all would have blown over.'

'Tell me the truth, Jane.' He was leaning over the table now, as well. 'Are you asking for my help because I'm your friend, or because I'm working as a model and it's some kind of strange status symbol for you?'

'Dude! I should have known you'd be hiding away canoodling with your new babe, you crafty dog!'

A chair scraped back and Thom threw himself down in it, blond hair flopping in his face. As usual, he looked as if he'd just stepped off a beach.

'Hi, Thom,' Jane said, and leaned quickly back in her chair. Jonny sat back, too.

'Don't pay any attention to me, my friends, you go right ahead and make all the goo-goo eyes at each other that you want. Jane, I'm stoked you like my man Jo—Jay.'

'Jane knows my real name,' Jonny told him.

Thom bobbed his head in delight. 'Excellent, that is excellent. You're really getting to know each other, huh?' He patted Jane's hand. 'I've been telling Jonny he needs a good woman to lighten him up, and I'm glad I was the person to introduce you.'

'Yes, it was quite a fateful lunch, wasn't it?' Jane smiled at Thom, with only the smallest of glances at Jonny to gauge his reaction.

'Written in the stars,' Thom agreed.

Thom didn't appear to be going anywhere until he'd done his full share of congratulating the two of them on their so-called relationship.

'Would you like a drink, Thom?' Jonny asked.

'I'd kill for a beer, dude. Make sure it's cold, though.'

'This is a café, Thom.'

'Oh. Yeah, okay, a macchiato, thanks. So, Jane, tell me what you love about our friend Jonny here.'

Jonny paused halfway out of his chair. He'd offered Thom a drink so that he could walk away and gather his thoughts for a minute, but now he wasn't sure that he wanted this conversation to go on without him.

Thom glanced at him and made shooing gestures with his hands. 'Go get out of here. I'm conferring with your girlfriend.'

'"Girlfriend" is perhaps a little—'

'Your red-hot babe friend, then. Go away.'

He went. All the way to the counter he kept his ears pricked, trying to hear Jane and Thom's conversation over the buzz of the café and the whoosh of the coffee machine. He didn't have much luck.

And what, precisely, did he want to hear, anyway? he wondered as he paid for Thom's drink. Did he want to make sure that Jane wasn't going ahead with the 'pretending to date' thing without his consent?

Or did he want to hear something that Jane loved about him?

He nearly spilled the macchiato all over his T-shirt in his haste to get back to the table. Jane was smiling and blushing and Thom was grinning and nodding in that 'all is cool with the world' way he had.

'What are you two talking about?' Jonny couldn't stop himself asking as he put the coffee down in front of his agent/friend and sat in his chair again.

Thom clapped him on the shoulder. 'Dude, you are one lucky man.' He took a swig of his macchiato and grimaced. 'Sugar,' he said, and got up and loped to the counter.

'Don't worry,' Jane said as soon as Thom was out of earshot. 'I didn't give away any secrets. We've been talking about your career, that's all.'

'And how devastatingly attractive you are,' Thom added, from halfway across the room.

'Hmmph.' Jonny covered up his disappointment by drinking his coffee, which was, by now, almost cold.

'Anyway, I'm sorry to interrupt your little cosy date thing,' Thom continued, while he finished crossing to them and sat back down in his chair, dumping five or six packets of sugar on the table, 'but I was on the way to Jonny's hotel to take him out for a beer and get the skinny on how it went today and I saw the two of you in here. And I want to pick your brains about somebody you work with, Jane.'

'You mean Gary?'

Jane was too quick to say it, and Jonny swallowed bitter coffee.

It was back to Gary again. Everything came back to Gary, it seemed. Jane's work, her feelings, this charade she wanted him to take on.

She'd just broken up with the bloke, after all. And how could he, Jonny, compete with that? As well as he believed he knew Jane, as much as he cared about her, when it was all said and done, besides the years as kids and that one night of wild passion, he and Jane had an internet relationship. And Jane was impressed by him being a model.

Compared with years of living and working with Gary, what he and Jane had together had to be shallow.

His coffee tasted like stale jealousy.

Thom was shaking his head, though. 'No, I mean your art person, who was at the shoot yesterday. Amy. She's hot, man. Is she seeing anybody?'

'No, I don't think so.'

'Awesome. Tell me all about her.' Thom leaned back in his chair as if it were a hammock.

'She's a very good art director. Completely reliable, and very creative. I don't have any talent at the visual side of things myself, so it's wonderful to have her on my team. I was very impressed with her CV when she joined the company last year, and she's completely lived up to it.'

'Yeah, yeah, that's great. But what about her? What does she like, what kind of guy does she go for, what's her favourite food? Does she like boxers or briefs? Wine or cocktails?'

Jonny saw Jane blink a few times. He remembered what she'd said about not having any friends.

'Um,' she said, and the slightly lost look in her eyes made him want to hug her. 'I'm not sure about her favourite food or drink or underwear.'

'Anything, I'll take anything. Help me out here.'

'I know she's got a little girl, who's about six,' Jane said slowly. 'I think she's called Stacy.'

'Oh.'

Thom didn't say anything else, but his face fell and Jonny could see his mind working. Thom's conception of a 'hot babe' probably didn't include her having a six-year-old daughter.

'And she's really nice. Amy, I mean. I haven't met Stacy, though I've seen her photo on Amy's desk. Amy's divorced.' Jane's brow furrowed. 'Or maybe they were never married. No, I think they're divorced.'

Thom's face was getting gloomier and gloomier, and Jane was obviously feeling awkward. Jonny opened his mouth to say something to rescue them both, but Jane beat him to it.

'Anyway,' she said, 'I know she's very excited about your party. She said she was definitely going to come and that she was impressed that you'd invited her yourself.'

Thom brightened. 'My party, yeah. It's going to be totally gnarly. The decadent decade, nineteen twenties theme all the way. Art nouveau building, beautiful people dressed like something out of *The Great Gatsby*. Awesome.'

Jonny had been to Thom's parties before, in California, always packed with glamorous people. He wasn't exactly the 'see and be seen' type himself, but there were usually interesting people there to talk to. And of course it was fun to see Thom in his element, talking with people, playing the host.

'Sounds great,' he said, privately hoping there would be lots of people there, so he could escape early and do some work on his book before its deadline without Thom noticing. *HTML for Utter Beginners* had been neglected lately, what with the photo shoots and the hot sex and the trying, and failing, to sort things out with Jane.

'And don't think you're going to slip off early and do some writing while I'm not looking, Clark Kent,' Thom said. 'I want to see you escorting your new lovely lady, fetching her drinks all night and whirling her around the dance floor and all that romantic stuff. You hear me?'

Jonny glanced over at Jane. Now was the time to come clean

about their lack of relationship, before Thom expected them to put on a show in front of everyone he'd invited to the party.

Which included Jane's ex, and his new girlfriend. And everybody who had seen him kissing Jane.

Jane's expressive grey eyes pleaded with him. Underneath the table, he felt her hand seek out his, and grip his fingers.

The touch of her skin, only this small extremity, was wonderful. He remembered holding her hand, sprinting down the pavement to his hotel and the most incredible experience he'd ever had in his life.

'I hear you,' he said. 'We'll be there.'

Jane checked her hair for at least the fourteenth time. She'd like to check her outfit, too, but for some reason Gary had owned the only full-length mirror in their flat and he'd taken it with him. The closest she could get to looking at how her rose-coloured drop-waisted silk dress fitted her was to stand on a chair in front of her mirrored bathroom cabinet and twist her body so that she could see the reflection of both her chest and her hips at the same time.

She didn't really need to look at her dress in the mirror. She'd only bought it this morning, and she'd looked at it plenty then, from every angle, trying to work out if it showed any humiliating bulges or gaps. It had taken quite a while before she'd decided that it was both concealing enough not to embarrass her and sexy enough to show the world that she was over Gary, happy with a new man, and on her way up.

She stood on her tiptoes and looked at her chest. Definite cleavage showing. If she were planning on trying to seduce Jonny—which she wasn't—she would say that this dress pretty much conformed to all of what he'd told her he liked in his date's clothing.

Not that she cared about that.

And then, of course, this dress was pink.

Jane forced herself away from the mirror. Second-guessing herself wasn't going to do her any good. She'd bought this dress especially for Thom's party, and any minute now Jonny was going to pick her up to escort her there, and, in any case, she didn't have anything else to wear. Her only other suitable dress was all wrinkled from being shoved up around her hips while she and Jonny...

She went right back to the mirror. Second-guessing herself about her dress was much better than thinking about the last time she'd dressed up for Jonny.

Perhaps if she put on a different shade of lipstick her dress wouldn't look quite so pink. She dug in her handbag to find the lipstick.

Jonny wasn't going to think that she was dressing up for him, anyway. She'd made herself quite clear on that point: they were friends, and that was it. She was glad that he'd agreed to go along with the act that they were seeing each other, but he definitely understood it was an act.

He hadn't called her, or emailed her, or sent her any more flowers; he was reserving his attentions for public display. When she'd visited the photographer's studio this morning to see how the last day of the shoot was going, he'd greeted her with a warm smile and a kiss on the lips that was equally warm, but over nearly as soon as it began.

She pursed her lips to check the effect of the lipstick. It had been a brief kiss, but an effective one. She'd seen it register with the photographer and his assistants.

And it had certainly affected her.

As had the arm he'd casually draped around her waist while speaking to her, and the long looks he'd given her with those deep blue eyes.

All of them purely for show.

Jane found a tissue in her bag and wiped off the lipstick and put the first one back on again. She didn't think either one of them made any difference: her dress was still the pinkest thing she'd ever worn and she was pretty sure she looked like a big fluffy stick of candyfloss.

And she was almost as sure that this boyfriend act wasn't saving her friendship with Jonny. Because if they were still friends he would have emailed her as he had nearly every other day of their friendship, wouldn't he?

Her bell rang. Quickly she stuffed lipsticks and tissue back into her handbag and went to answer the door.

Jonny stood in the hallway. And for a moment, all she could do was stare.

He wore a black suit and a crisp light blue shirt and brighter blue tie, but on Jonny these articles of clothing stopped being merely clothes and were vehicles for his gorgeousness. His suit emphasised his broad shoulders, his lean waist; his shirt and tie made his eyes still bluer. His hair was pushed back from his face in a calmer version of the messy hairdo the stylist had given him for the photo shoot, and even that showed off his high cheek-bones, the perfect shape of his jaw.

And, as always, he smelled of warm cotton and Jonny, familiar and yet new.

'You look wonderful, Jane,' he said, and only then did she realise that he'd been looking back at her.

'You don't think it's too pink?' she blurted, because that was the only thing she could think to say. Her brains appeared to be entirely muddled by the idea that she was going to be spending the evening with a man who looked and smelled and, God forgive her, felt and tasted as incredible as Jonny did.

'I don't think anything could possibly be too pink,' he said. 'It's a good colour on you.'

'It's very girly.'

'Which fits, because, last time I checked, you were defi-nitely a girl.'

With that, her circulatory system, which seemed to have been on pause since she'd opened the door, started up again and she felt the blood rush to her face. 'Uh, come in.'

He stepped past her and stood in her living room, surveying the space. 'Nice flat.'

Jane closed the door behind him, suddenly becoming aware that this was only the second time since they were eleven years old that the two of them had been totally alone in a room together, with no observers.

Except this time, she wasn't going to allow herself to touch him.

'Thanks,' she said, trying to sound nonchalant.

He nodded at the empty space in the centre of the room. 'Have you got something against furniture?'

'Gary took it. Would you like a drink before we go?'

He didn't seem to have heard the question; instead he was looking at her with that typical Jonny kindness.

'I'm sorry, Jane. I would have thought the bastard would at least have left you somewhere to sit down.'

'I can get new furniture.'

'Yes, the furniture will be easy to replace.' There was something harsher than kindness in his emphasis on the word 'furniture'. He wandered across the hardwood floor to her desk, set against one of the unfinished brick walls. He touched her closed laptop lightly, and then laid his hand on the back of her chair. 'This is where you talk with me.'

'Uh-huh.' And that was exactly where she'd been sitting when they'd had their last online conversation. About sex. And where she'd been sitting when she'd waited in vain for him to email her, yesterday and today.

'You were wonderful at the photo shoot,' she said, to change the subject.

He looked up from his scrutiny of her desk. 'Are you talking about my modelling, or my acting?'

'Both.'

He nodded and reached into the pocket of his suit. 'I have something for you,' he said, and pulled out a small white box.

She was nervous enough to fumble slightly opening it. Inside, on a bit of velvet, rested a silver necklace with a fine chain and a pendant in the shape of a heart.

'Oh, Jonny, it's lovely,' she said. She touched the heart, and then her own chest, between her breasts where the pendant would lie. 'You didn't need to give me anything like this.'

'It's strategy.' He took the box from her hands and lifted out the necklace. She turned around and held up her hair so he could fasten the chain around her neck. The warmth of his hands feathered across her nape, and she felt his breath on her skin as he spoke.

'What you do, is you fiddle with the necklace all night, and then whenever anybody comments on it, you say that I gave it to you. It should be convincing.' He turned her around and looked at her.

She touched the heart, so close to where her own was beating. The necklace was a tool, then. To achieve what she'd said she wanted.

It was still just as beautiful, but it suddenly seemed less precious.

'You shouldn't have done that,' she said, hoping he was looking at the pendant, and not how his near-touch had hardened her nipples underneath her dress. 'You're trying to save money, aren't you?'

'Some things are worth spending money for.'

He raised his eyes to her face, and in the momentary heat she saw there she knew he'd noticed what his touch did to her.

Then he was neutral-faced, a man she couldn't quite read. 'Don't worry about anything, Jane. I haven't forgotten our plan. I intend to be the perfect boyfriend tonight. The model boy-friend.' There was the slightest hint of bitterness in how he said the last three words.

But then he smiled, like Jonny, and held out his arm for her to take. 'Let's go and put on our show.'

CHAPTER EIGHT

'Stop here, please, mate.'

The cab pulled up to the side of the road several metres from the front of the building where Thom was having his party. Jane gathered her wrap and her bag, looking at Jonny questioningly.

'Strategy,' he told her again. 'Stay here for a minute.' He got out of the cab, paid the driver, and went around to open her door for her. 'May I?' he said, offering her his hand to help her out of the cab.

'I don't need help,' she said, but she couldn't resist taking his hand anyway. Fifteen minutes in a cab next to Jonny, her leg just brushing his when the uneven London street jostled them, was enough to tempt a saint's patience.

He was warm and steady. She stepped down from the cab and saw a flash. Jonny pulled her close to him and slipped an arm around her waist as something flashed again.

Jane felt dizzy from the lights and Jonny holding her. 'What's going on?'

'Thom usually gets someone to tip off the paparazzi about his parties,' he murmured in her ear. 'We're relatively small fry, but we might make a couple of the glossies. Smile—it's good publicity for your company and for our relationship.'

He brushed her hair back and gave her a kiss on the temple before he twined his fingers around hers and began to walk with her down the pavement.

Dazed, Jane held onto Jonny's hand and looked around for a camera to smile at. There were quite a few, all pointed at them as they traversed the distance between the cab and the party. The route Jonny had chosen brought them directly into the path of the photographers.

Strategy, indeed.

She glanced over at Jonny. He was smiling, confident, gorgeous. Of course, he was used to cameras. She tried her best to look like someone who belonged holding hands with him. That was, like someone other than herself.

They reached the door, flanked by large bouncers, and Jonny gave their names. He led her through a short corridor and into a wonderland.

The interior of the art nouveau building was all elegant white lines and tall thin stained-glass windows. Crystal chandeliers in the shapes of flowers cascaded from the ceiling. But the people, dressed in dark suits and glittering flapper-style dresses, outshone the surroundings.

Thom approached them, his arms and smile stretched wide. He was wearing a dinner jacket and a Hawaiian shirt, a fashion combination that Jane would associate more with teenage boys than a millionaire models' agent, but on Thom, as usual, it worked.

'How's it going, my lovebird friends?' he asked, flinging his arms around them both.

'Brilliant,' Jane managed, narrowly avoiding getting a mouthful of shaggy blond hair. 'This party is amazing,' she said when Thom let them go.

Thom shrugged. 'Not bad. It's the people that make it beautiful. You look gorgeous, woman.'

A compliment from Thom didn't make Jane blush; she'd worked with him several times and she knew that, while he was sincere, he was also generous.

'So do you,' she said. It was a lame compliment, but Thom beamed as if she'd just given him the moon.

'Thanks, babe, but I don't have that new love glow like you do.' A little cloud passed his sunny face. 'I haven't seen your friend Amy yet—did she decide not to come?'

'She'll definitely be here,' Jane told him. 'She hasn't talked about anything but this party for days.'

In fact, she'd been in Jane's office that morning, worrying

about her clothes and her daughter, who'd already been spending way too much time with a babysitter because of the extra hours Amy had been putting in on designing the Franco cologne advertisements. Jane hadn't been able to be much help, but she'd reassured Amy as best she could. It was almost like the girly bonding Jane had always vaguely hoped for with Amy.

'Okay, okay, cool. Listen, you need one of these.' He dipped into a gold-covered box on a table next to him and handed them each a glittery disposable camera. 'I want plenty of memories of tonight.'

'I think we're all going to remember this night for a very long time,' Jonny said, taking a camera. 'Smile,' he said to Jane, and clicked a photo of her, though she was pretty sure she had her mouth half open and her eyes half shut.

'No porno pics, now,' Thom said to them with a wink, and then he turned to greet the next set of guests.

Jonny took her hand again and led her forward into the glittering room. At first glance, Jane thought that about half the people in the room looked familiar. At second glance, she realised that was because the half she recognised were famous—and the other half probably were, too, only she wouldn't know because she didn't have much time to watch television or movies or read celebrity magazines.

'Smile,' she heard somebody say, and Jonny pulled her quickly to his side and pressed a kiss to her cheek as a camera snapped and flashed. The camera owner, a small blonde, giggled at them and moved on to take some more photos.

'Perfect,' Jonny murmured to her.

'I'm not sure I like having my picture taken so much,' she said, twisting her head around to check if someone else was going to ambush them.

'It's good,' Jonny said, though his voice was a bit grim. 'We've got documentary evidence. If we play it right, we can have our photo snapped together dozens of times tonight, every time being a perfect couple. Isn't that the sort of thing you want?'

'I'm—' She clapped her mouth shut as another flash went off near them. She'd been about to say she wasn't sure of that, either.

But then that was ridiculous. Showing the world that she and Jonny were a perfect couple was exactly what she'd planned.

'Jane,' someone said to her, and this time she recognised the voice as well as the face: Hasan, from the office, with his wife, Sharon.

Jane greeted them with the customary air kisses on both cheeks. 'So good to see you,' she said, and then turned to present Jonny. 'Hasan, Sharon, this is Jo—'

'Jay Richard,' Jonny quickly and smoothly interrupted, and shook hands with the couple. Jane bit her lip at her near-mistake.

'You're the model working on the Franco cologne campaign, aren't you?' Hasan was acting merely polite and professional, but Jane caught an extra whiff of interest. Of course, he was the one who'd picked up on tension between her and Gary the other day…and in the office it was open season on gossip about the break-up and Jane's new relationship.

Sharon confirmed her thoughts by stepping slightly aside with her and saying, in a low voice, 'I was so sorry to hear that it didn't work out between you and Gary.'

'Thank you,' Jane said. Though she wasn't sure what one was supposed to say in this situation. 'Thank you' didn't seem quite appropriate, but then again nor did, 'It's none of your business,' since Jane's love life seemed to be being conducted in public and she couldn't exactly blame people for talking about it.

'Your date is very handsome,' Sharon continued.

Irritation flared through Jane, though again she couldn't say why, because that comment was precisely the reason that she was at this party. She bit off the 'thank you' that seemed to be required again, and merely nodded.

Sharon seemed to take that as encouragement to greater intimacy. She put her hand on Jane's arm and leaned closer, her voice lower.

'What's it like to date a model? I'll bet you get envious looks from every woman in the room.'

'There is a bit of that,' Jane replied, only just overcoming her irritation enough to avoid pulling away from Sharon's insistent grip. She'd been to social occasions with Sharon before, once or twice as couples with her and Gary and Sharon and Hasan. Mostly Jane preferred to talk with the men, with whom she could discuss business. But of course she'd been expected to talk to Sharon, as the other female. As she remembered, her conversations with Sharon had been purely superficial, chat about things such as the latest big news item or the weather or property prices in London. There had never been anything as personal as this.

But then maybe that was how female friendships worked, on an exchange of gossip and confidences. Jane smiled and tried for the same bright intimacy as Sharon.

'You must be used to admiring looks yourself,' she said. 'Hasan's a very good-looking man.'

Sharon's face immediately closed. 'Yes, he is,' she said, unmistakable hostility in her voice. She dropped Jane's arm and put her own arm in Hasan's, breaking eye contact with Jane to look lovingly at her husband instead as he chatted with Jonny.

So that was it. It was common knowledge that Jane had hopped from one relationship to another with an incredibly good-looking man, and therefore she was a man-hungry threat.

What on earth was she supposed to do? Women didn't want to be her friend when she was in a steady relationship…and now that she was supposed to be excitingly dating, she was equally un-befriendable.

Jane sighed. Better to be a threat than an object of pity. She put her smile back on as Jonny wound up his conversation with Hasan, which Sharon had now joined, and wandered off with him when he took her hand again.

'That went well,' Jonny murmured to her.

'Exactly according to plan,' she replied.

He slanted a look at her. 'You don't seem very happy about it.'

'It's—' She sighed again. 'Oh, I don't know. I just don't know what people expect of me, that's all.'

'They expect you to be happy,' Jonny said firmly. 'So we'll give them what they want.'

'But I don't—'

I don't know how to be friends with anybody. It seemed like such a pathetic admission to make.

'You don't what?'

She tried half of it. 'I'm not good with women. I'm not really sure how to behave with them so they'll like me.'

'Men are easier?' He asked it with a tilt of his head and a half-smile, as if he found the idea amusing.

'Yes. I mean, look at Thom. What you see is what you get with him. He tells you exactly what he expects of you, and he's happy when you're happy.'

'Yes. But Thom's not exactly your usual bloke.'

'True.' She tried to think of how to explain. 'I think it's from having four brothers. I've always been more comfortable around men, if I can deal with them as equals. They don't hide what they want.'

'I wouldn't count on it,' Jonny said.

He'd sounded as if he was saying it more to himself than her, but she responded to the comment anyway.

'You're probably right. I don't really know what men want, either.'

'Look out, camera.'

Jonny swung her into his arms and without any warning, he was kissing her.

Her body reacted before her mind even knew what was happening. She arched up into him and buried her fingers in the soft hair at the nape of his neck, parting her lips under his and feeling a delicious shudder go through her as his tongue touched the inside of her lip, and his mouth took control of every nerve ending in her body.

There was a click. Jonny held the kiss for a second more, and then he let her go.

Fortunately his arms were still around her, or else she would have tottered. The room was swaying and he was the only steady thing in it.

'That was perfect,' he said.

It was more than perfect, she thought. Tender, passionate, and drenched with desire. She lifted her lips towards his for another kiss. One wasn't enough. Never enough, when it was this good, and she and Jonny wanted each other so much.

And then she remembered.

It was perfect because it had been caught on camera.

She hesitated, her head tilted towards his, her arms still around his neck, her mouth offered up to him. What was real here, and what was fake? Because you couldn't fake a kiss like that, could you?

'Jonny,' she said, and searched his blue eyes for a sign.

He put his fingers on her lips, so gently that it would seem to anyone else that it was a caress, part of their kiss.

'No, Jane. Don't call me that.' His voice was low and smooth. 'I'm Jay Richard tonight, remember? The model you had wild sex with on the first date. Not the normal man you've known for years.'

He let her go, and stepped back from her. She noticed that his clothing was unrumpled.

'I could use a drink,' he said. 'What would you like? Champagne?'

She nodded, and he was gone.

Oh, what a mess. Jane hauled in a shaky breath and leaned against a fortuitously placed column to prop up her unsteady, lust-ridden body.

She really had no clue what men wanted, if Jonny could walk away from a kiss like that with nothing more than a reminder to her about what to call him.

She looked around the room. It was full of beautiful people, beautifully dressed, laughing and talking and having a good time.

Were they all putting on a show, too? Or did they have something that Jane lacked, something that let them connect with others, stop being self-conscious, stop second-guessing and just *be*?

Jane bit her lip and fiddled with the smooth heart-shaped pendant on her chest. It was warm from her skin, most likely because Jonny's touch and his kiss were heating her up.

'Jane.'

She recognised this voice, too; it was Amy, breathless from hurrying across the room, wearing a man's tuxedo that had been altered to fit her small, curvy body. Despite the male clothing she looked incredibly feminine, with patent leather high heels on her feet and her hair piled in a jumble of glossy curls on her head. She held a half-full champagne flute of orange juice in her hand.

'Can I lean here with you?' she asked. 'These shoes are killing me already. And if I sit down I'm afraid nobody is going to talk with me.'

Jane made room beside her at the column and Amy joined her, leaning her back up against it with a sound of relief.

'This is all so overwhelming, isn't it?' Amy continued. 'The last party I went to was a birthday bash for one of Stacy's school friends. It was in McDonald's.' She surveyed the room. 'This is very grown-up. And have you seen the clothes on these people? Lots of them work in the fashion world and, boy, don't they look it?'

'I like your outfit,' Jane said honestly. 'It suits you.'

'Oh. Thanks. I ended up ditching the thing I bought and going for this instead. I thought I'd be more comfortable, but all I can think of is the fact that I bought it for twelve pounds fifty on the Portobello Road four years ago and that it's held together with safety pins.'

Jane laughed, and Amy grinned back at her. Apparently she wasn't touchy about her worries.

'I keep on thinking about looking like candyfloss,' Jane admitted.

'No, you suit pink. It brings out your skin tone; you could wear it more. Besides, that's not candyfloss, that's rose.'

'Is there a difference?'

Amy rolled her eyes. 'And this is why I'm a lowly art person while you're the boss.'

'And probably why I don't wear pink more often.'

Amy nodded and took a drink of her orange juice, looking around the room again. 'Jane, you know what Thom Erikson's like, don't you?'

'I've worked with him several times,' Jane answered. 'Why?'

'Oh, he was just so nice when he invited me to the party. He seemed really friendly, you know. But tonight he basically said hello to me and then that was it. I was wondering if that's the way he is, or if I'd done something wrong.'

Jane only knew at that moment that she'd finally relaxed a bit, because she could feel the difference when she instantly tensed. Thom's behaviour was her fault, because she'd told him about Stacy. Some friend she was.

'I don't think you've done anything wrong,' she said.

'Maybe he's busy with his guests.'

Jane debated whether she should tell Amy that Thom had said she was a 'hot babe', but then decided it would only make things worse. 'Maybe you should find him and talk with him.'

Amy seemed to brighten a little. 'Yeah, maybe. It can't hurt, right?' She gestured towards Jonny, who was crossing the room towards them, a glass of champagne in each hand. 'I should definitely take your advice. You're my hero at the moment. You didn't let yourself get down after your break-up with Gary, you went right out there and grabbed life with both hands!'

Jane squirmed. 'I wouldn't say that was exactly heroic.'

'Of course it is. I never would have the guts up to go out with a model. I mean, look at me—I can hardly get it together to talk to a millionaire!'

Amy laughed but Jane couldn't really share her mirth. Two minutes ago she'd been feeling comfortable, and now she was returning Amy's easy confidences with the same lie she was giving to everyone else in the room.

'Hi, Amy,' Jonny said as he approached them. He handed one glass of champagne to Jane and offered the other to Amy, who shook her head. 'Are you enjoying the party?'

'Yes, very much, thanks, Jay. Jane was just giving me a little pep talk.'

'It wasn't much of a pep talk, I'm afraid.' Jane twisted her necklace around her fingers, tight enough to hurt.

'It was exactly what I needed. That's a pretty necklace.'

'Oh. Thanks. Jo—Jay gave it to me.' She couldn't help but catch Jonny's eye as she said it, and she saw his slight nod of approval. It made her twist her fingers even more tightly.

'Good taste,' Amy told Jonny.

'Definitely.' Jonny put his arm around Jane's shoulders and held her close to his side.

'So will you try talking with him?' Jane asked, stiffening a little in Jonny's embrace. Right now it seemed too…possessive. As if by pretending to be having a relationship with her, he was pretending to own her, too.

'Yes,' Amy said decisively, and put down her juice glass on the tray of a passing waiter. 'I'm going to go find him now. Wish me luck.'

'Good luck,' Jane said, and Jonny echoed her.

'What are we wishing her luck for?' he asked, watching Amy stride purposefully across the room in her black suit and high heels.

'Talking with your Californian friend. I think he's avoiding her.' Jane took a long drink of her champagne, feeling the bubbles in her nose and throat, where they did absolutely nothing to relax her. 'Did I say that men are more straightforward than women? Because I was utterly wrong.' She swigged again.

'Jane.' For the third time tonight, she recognised the voice saying her name. And this one was the one she'd been dreading.

She swallowed her champagne, took a deep breath, and turned to face Gary and Kathleen.

CHAPTER NINE

HE'D never seen Gary before, but Jonny knew who he was instantly from the way that Jane's body tensed before she faced him.

Gary was good-looking. He was tall and fit and had brown hair and eyes and a masculine dimple in his chin, like Cary Grant. Jonny felt his stomach tighten and he realised he hadn't given much thought to what Gary looked like.

He drew Jane a little closer to his side, though she had pulled herself up so straight that it was difficult to do.

'Hello, Gary,' she said, and he found himself searching for some warmth in her voice. There wasn't much there beyond civility, but he was still bothered. Bothered that she was suppressing her feelings, bothered that this man was still so important to her that she'd arranged this whole charade for his benefit, bothered that he himself cared that Gary was attractive.

And he'd said that appearances didn't matter.

'This must be the model,' Gary said, holding out his hand, and Jonny was bothered by that, too.

'Jay Richard,' he said, shaking Gary's hand, and wishing he'd been quick enough to get his introduction in first. Gary gripped his hand hard, with sharp stabs of shakes. A challenge, not a greeting.

'The face of Franco cologne,' Gary said. 'I hope you're wearing it.'

'I'm afraid not, but I've got boxes of the stuff,' Jay replied as pleasantly as he could. 'I'd be happy to give you a bottle or six.'

'This is Kathleen Dunne,' Gary said, dropping Jonny's hand and bringing his date forward with a hand in the small of her back.

Kathleen had swapped her waitress uniform for party gear:

full sex-kitten make-up, skin-tight black dress and stiletto heels. It looked as if he and Jane weren't the only ones putting on a show tonight.

Jonny wasn't interested in what Kathleen thought about this whole situation, though. He watched Jane as she nodded to Kathleen with a chilly smile, and glanced at Gary just in time to catch him giving Jane the once-over, from her softly waving hair to her drop-waisted silk dress, demure but still sexy in a way that more overt clothing could never be. And her shoes, fine leather high-heeled sandals that showed a hint of Jane's toes, painted rose to match her dress.

He'd heard Gary liked shoes. And Jonny would bet the advance on every book he'd written that, despite the sexpot by his side, Gary still wanted Jane.

His hand tightened on Jane's waist.

'Are you enjoying the party?' he asked, because although his instinct was to throw Jane over his shoulder and beat his chest in Tarzan style, that was probably not anyone's idea of perfect boyfriend behaviour.

'Thom's parties are always fantastic,' Gary said, and Jonny didn't even have to look at Jane to know that her eyes were narrowing at the remark. She'd said she'd never been to one of Thom's parties; apparently Gary had been making appearances without her.

'I loved the one where he hired the London Eye,' Kathleen piped up. 'There were all these lights? And the view was astounding.'

Jane's intake of breath was only just perceptible. Jonny's stomach got tighter with anger. He wanted to hold Jane, take away her pain at this little nasty evidence of betrayal, but if he tightened his grip any more he was going to hurt her.

He turned to her instead, because the sooner they got away from these poisonous people, the better he was going to feel. 'I don't think we need to—'

Her face was set and composed and he saw that Jane was going to be damned if she let anyone see that she was hurt by them.

Jonny's heart twisted and all at once he remembered a hundred incidents from his childhood where his father had been angry with a customer at their bed and breakfast who had been treating his wife with less than the total respect that he'd believed she'd deserved. Every time, a look from his wife would quell him and Jonathan Cole Senior would stand by, a strong near reassurance, as Naomi Cole had dealt with her customers with quiet dignity.

He swallowed his anger. 'I'm enjoying working on the Franco cologne campaign,' he said to Gary. 'I'm not an expert on advertising but I think the design is striking, and from what I've seen Jane has done some very clever copywriting.'

'Jane is extremely talented,' Gary said. Jonny's estimation of him went up slightly because he said it with no hesitation at all. 'Giovanni Franco's team have been impressed with her work, and he is not an easy client to please.'

'I'm a lucky man to have met her,' Jonny said, and gave Jane the smile and the look that said plainly how much he was crazy about her, and that was only a lie because of circumstances, not of feeling. She returned it, though he could see the subtle hints of strain around her eyes.

Kathleen had been shifting from side to side on her stilettos, obviously unhappy with the turn of the conversation to Jane-appreciation. 'What are you two doing over the weekend?' she asked. 'Gary and I are flying to Milan.'

'Buying shoes?' Jane muttered, and Jonny interposed.

'Jane and I are getting away as well,' he said. 'The shoot's done and we thought we'd celebrate by going somewhere remote and romantic for the weekend.'

'Yes, I thought it was time I took a break from work for once,' Jane said, without a trace of surprise at their sudden fictional weekend date. 'I hear a man likes it when a woman takes the time to get to know him.'

He wasn't exactly sure why, but that seemed to hit home with Gary, whose handsome face flushed.

'Well, that calls for a celebration,' Gary said. 'Why don't I track down one of those bottles of champagne that are making the rounds?'

Kathleen had latched her arm around Gary's in a death grip. 'I'll help you, darling,' she said, and steered him, without any subtlety, away from Jane and Jonny towards the centre of the room.

Jane raised her glass to her lips and drained it. Then she took Jonny's glass from the nearby table where he'd placed it to shake Gary's hand and drained that, too.

'Can we get out of here for a minute?' she asked, and the strain he'd only seen traces of before in her eyes was so stark that he immediately walked with her in the other direction from Gary and Kathleen, towards a set of French windows that apparently led to a balcony. She grabbed another glass of champagne from a passing waiter before they stepped through the windows outside.

Until the evening air cooled his face, he didn't know just how heated up he'd been. The balcony ran nearly the length of the building, lit softly by lights of South Kensington. Jane went straight to the gracefully curled stone railing and leant her elbows against it, looking out at the view and taking a sip of champagne. Her bare shoulders looked narrow and fragile in the dim light.

He leant next to her. It was impossible to keep from brushing a stray curl back from her face. 'How are you doing?'

'Can we spend a few minutes not thinking about this whole girlfriend and boyfriend act thing? Just spend a few minutes being ourselves with each other?'

'No problem.'

'Good.' She took a deep breath, and let it out. He wasn't touching her but he could feel her relaxing a little bit. She breathed deeply again. Jonny leant next to her, looking outwards, letting her be.

'Do you remember how we used to climb trees?' she asked abruptly. 'How we used to hide from Paul and Dylan and Jez and Billy when they were teasing us?'

'And drop conkers on their heads.'

She nodded and he saw the beginnings of her first real smile of the night. 'You used to make me call you Tarzan.'

Jonny laughed. Maybe that earlier thought about slinging her over her shoulder hadn't come from nowhere after all. 'Me Tarzan, you Jane.'

'I liked it up in those trees. Do you remember the night we stayed up there until it got dark? We got in so much trouble.'

He remembered it perfectly. He'd been eleven and it had been only a few weeks before he'd moved up to the Lake District with his parents so they could start their first bed and breakfast. They'd stuffed their pockets full of biscuits and sat together straddling a branch, eating crumbs, the whole world beneath them.

As the sun had set Jane's every delicate feature had been bathed in pink. The inside of her lips had been in dark shadow, her eyes alight. He had an image in his head of her leaning back against the tree trunk, swinging her legs, tipping back her head and laughing at something they had said.

'I remember it,' he said. He didn't say what he was thinking: *You were the girl of my dreams.*

'What are your brothers up to, anyway?' he said instead.

'Paul and Jez are barristers. Dylan just accepted a promotion at his bank that means he'll be working in Hong Kong for the next couple of years. And Billy's had a very good offer from a multinational for his consulting company, but he's holding out for a better.'

'Wow. You all turned out high achievers, didn't you?'

'It's important for us to do well. I'm proud of them.'

'Any of them married? Kids?'

'Dylan has two sons. Boy children run in our family. Paul's wife Miranda is expecting, and if it turns out to be a girl I think every Miller in existence will go into shock. The last female Miller to be born was back in nineteen twenty-four.'

'Aside from you, of course.'

'Aside from me.'

He wondered if she'd actually forgotten to count herself. 'That must make you very special in your family.'

His eyes had adjusted to the light, and he could see her raise her eyebrows. 'It made me different, anyway. Though you must remember what I was like as a kid. I was a total tomboy.'

'You always seemed very female to me.'

The twist of her lips was so funnily vulnerable that he wanted to give her a hug. But he wasn't sure of the parameters of their touching in a friendly way, and he wanted so much more than that in any case that he kept his hands to himself now that they were in private.

She took a sip of her champagne. 'I never really said how sorry I am for your mother and what she's going through. I mean, I did, but I didn't know she was your mother at the time. If that makes sense.'

'It does. Thank you.'

'How is she doing? She was always so calm, I remember. Your house was very peaceful compared to mine full of brothers. I liked going over there.'

Jonny smiled, because he'd always liked going over to Jane's house because it had been so full of activity, and, most of all, Jane.

'It's hard to tell exactly how she's doing,' he said. 'I've seen her nearly every day since I've moved back to England, but she doesn't talk much. She never did; it was my father who was the expressive one.' He let out a laugh that was mirthless, despite his earlier fond memory. 'Except when he was keeping dark secrets, apparently.'

'If this campaign goes well and Giovanni Franco decides to extend it, it could be very lucrative for you,' Jane said. 'Maybe lucrative enough to pay off your debts.'

'Maybe.'

Jane put her champagne glass down on the stone balustrade and turned to face him. 'You should tell her.'

'Excuse me?'

Her chin was set. 'You should tell your mother about your father's debts. She deserves to know the truth.'

'Jane, I don't recall asking for your advice about this.'

'You're my friend and I'm giving it to you. I don't think it's right for you to keep the truth from her, even if it's bad news. She's a grown woman and should know what's happening to her.'

He felt his hand tightening on the stone railing. 'I don't think you're in a good position to talk about getting the truth out in the open, considering why we're here tonight.'

'My situation and your mother's are completely different.'

'Are they? It seems as if I'm being dragged into deception by both situations, because I want to do the best thing for someone who I care about.'

'Jonny, I'm just your friend. This is your mother we're talking about.'

You're not just my friend.

He bit back the words, because they were pointless. Because this relationship was going no further than this ridiculous act.

'I can't tell her,' he said instead, doggedly. 'It would destroy her image of my father. I need—'

I need someone to still think of my father as a good man, because otherwise it's too unbearable. Again, he couldn't say it. There was the truth, and then there was the big truth.

'It would hurt her too much,' he finished.

'But you're doing exactly the same thing to her that your father did. Hiding things. I know you want to protect her, Jonny, but if you care about somebody you can't deceive them.'

'And where does that put you and Gary?'

She opened her mouth, her eyes wide with surprise and shock, because he'd spat out the question.

'I—'

'Whoa there, lovebirds. If you think you're going to fly away, you've got another think coming.'

Why did Thom always choose the worst possible moment to appear? Jonny swallowed, relaxed his shoulders, and turned to his friend. Thom was holding a bottle of champagne and was accompanied by Amy, who was looking cheerful and chic.

'Just having a breather,' Jonny said.

'Have some champagne while you're breathing.' Thom filled up Jane's glass to the rim, noticed Jonny didn't have a glass, and offered him the bottle. Jonny shook his head.

'You two look very cosy out here,' Amy said.

Jane took a gulp of her champagne. 'Not so cosy that friends aren't welcome,' she said, and Jonny, who was attuned to every one of her moods whether he wanted to be or not, thought he caught a look of guilt.

'Dude, you're not drinking. Let's go find you a glass.' Thom grabbed hold of Jonny's sleeve and more or less dragged him across the balcony towards the French doors, leaving the women to talk to each other.

'What's up, Thom?'

Thom's eyes were wide and his face looked half panicked. 'Dude, I really like that woman.'

'That's wonderful.'

Thom shook his head violently. 'No, it's totally, totally bad.'

'Why? She seems like a great woman, and she likes you, too.'

'Okay. Let's put it this way. You know how you were joking that I haven't had sex since the last leap year? Well, it wasn't that far off the truth. I've been dating, you know, having fun, just skating along. Of course I'm a regular guy, and if sex looks like it's going to happen, you know, you usually take it, but lately it's seemed like too much of a hassle, like it's easier to just—just—'

'Skate along?'

'Yeah. Skate. And the thing is, about Amy, is I'm thinking that she's not skateable.'

Jonny removed the champagne bottle from Thom's fingers. He wasn't sure if his friend should be in swigging distance of alcohol right now.

'So what you're trying to say is that you think if you get involved with this woman, it's going to be a serious thing? You're maybe going to fall in love with her and that's scaring you?'

'Yeah. Yeah, that's it. Exactly.'

Jonny couldn't help glancing back at the railing, where Jane stood talking with Amy. He was angry with her, for this situation, for not sharing his emotions, for questioning his feelings about his own family. But his entire body and soul wanted nothing more than to go over there and take her in his arms.

He put the champagne bottle down on the floor. Booze was a bad idea for him, too. His judgement was already impaired enough.

'So it looks like we have two choices, mate,' he said to Thom. 'We can turn around right now and run out of here as fast as we can.'

'Yeah. Yeah. And what's the other choice?'

'We can go and ask Jane and Amy to dance.'

Thom's eyes were haunted. 'What should we do?'

'What do you want to do?'

'I want to dance with her.' Thom kicked the floor. 'Dammit.'

'Me too.' And once he touched her, it was going to take all of his control not to forget his anger, not to show her exactly how hopelessly in love with her he was. 'Also dammit.'

Thom gripped Jonny's shoulder. 'Okay. Let's go over and ask them. I tell you what, though, my friend. We are totally screwed.'

CHAPTER TEN

'COME on, girls, let's dance.'

Jane and Amy had leant against the balcony together, looking out at the view and drinking champagne and sharing easy chatter about Pearce Grey and Amy's career before she'd been hired there. Fortunately, Amy hadn't brought up Jane's relationship with Jonny again; Jane was feeling guilty enough about deceiving her earlier. At Thom's voice, they both turned around.

'Is this you trying to sweep us up off our feet with charm and wit?' There was laughter in Amy's voice.

Thom scratched the back of his head. 'I guess I could make up a poem.'

'No need.' Amy linked her arm with his. 'I thought you'd never ask.'

Jonny was standing very still beside Thom, and his face was grim. As Amy and Thom headed towards the French doors back into the party he approached her.

'Let's go dance,' he said.

'I think that's even less charming than what Thom said,' Jane replied. He was serious, and she could see the anger he'd shown when they'd talked about his mother simmering under the surface.

'I only need to be charming in public.' He held his arm out towards the party. 'Come on, it's time to start acting again.'

Jane hesitated. Something had changed from their comfortable, comforting friendship of a few minutes ago. It was even different from their play-acting in front of Hasan and Gary. This Jonny's face was set in harsh lines, and he made no effort to touch her or to meet her eyes.

'I don't really know how to dance,' she said.

'There's no grace required. All we have to do is to show everybody that we're completely in love. Should be easy.' He held out his hand to her, though the pose was formal. 'So, Jane, would you care to dance with me?'

She put her hand in his and let him guide her back into the party.

The air inside was warm and close; the lights and the dresses and people glittered. The band was playing a song she vaguely recognised: slow, sweet, and old-fashioned, with a rhythm like a heartbeat. The minute they were inside, Jonny drew her a little closer so that her hip bumped against him as they walked to the dance floor.

Thom and Amy were already there, Thom's hand on her hip and her head resting on his shoulder. Their suits were similar, but Thom's light hair bobbed over Amy's dark curls. They didn't appear to be speaking; Amy had her eyes closed and a dreamy smile on her face, and Thom was looking down at her, his expression faintly alarmed.

Jonny guided Jane to a spot near them and he pulled her close.

'Just follow my lead,' he whispered to her. He put his hand on her waist, and Jane could feel the warmth of his palm and fingers through the silk of her dress. His hand made her feel smaller, more delicate. She curled her arm around his neck, brushing her fingertips against his bare skin between his collar and his hair, and rested her other hand in his.

Their bodies weren't quite touching, but the warmth and reality of Jonny pressed against her entire front. Her breasts were a fraction of an inch from his chest. They might as well have been plastered all over him, because they felt tingling and alive and tight just from being near him.

She remembered the friction of his skin against her breasts as he had taken her, up against that wall. So hard and yet so tender.

He smiled down at her and nobody else in the room would have known it wasn't real.

Then again, nobody else in the room could see his eyes.

'Do what I do, in reverse,' he murmured to her, and began to dance.

Jane hadn't been kidding when she'd said she didn't know how to dance. She'd hardly even been to a school disco. She'd danced at her two brothers' weddings, but only to the fast songs.

Never like this. Not slowly, close to a man, feeling his breath on the side of her face, hearing the rustle of his clothes even louder than the music.

'You have to move your feet, Jane,' Jonny said to her.

'How?'

'Like this.' His grip on her waist tightened a little, and he began to move, first backwards and then to the side, in time with the music, pulling her gently along with him. They were small steps, movement for the sake of movement rather than for any point, and Jane found it easy to follow.

'How'd you learn to dance?' she asked.

'I'm making it up as I go along.'

She felt safe enough from falling over to glance up at his face. 'You're good at it.'

'It's not a complex dance. All it requires is for us to be close to each other and appear to be moving in harmony.' He smiled at her again, and again it didn't reach his eyes.

Jane couldn't move for a second, and her leg bumped against Jonny's.

She'd moved in harmony with him once. Their lips kissing, their bodies hungry for each other. Where had it gone?

The high heels, the dress, his hands on her, all the people and the music and the lights. It was all wrong, a fake. Not who she really was.

She pulled back from Jonny. 'I can't do this.'

'Shh.' He dipped his head and nuzzled her temple as he spoke. 'People are watching, Jane. You can do this. You'll be fine. Just relax and follow me and the music. If we're lucky some people will still have film in their cameras.'

Photographs, of her at this moment, her body yearning for Jonny, and the two of them further apart than they'd ever been. 'Jonny—'

Jonny stopped her lips with a kiss. It was both gentle and controlling and Jane felt herself helplessly responding to it, wanting more.

'I'm Jay,' he said against her mouth. 'And the two of us are in love.'

He began to dance with her again, except now he pulled her closer against him, so that she had no choice but to lay her head against his shoulder.

She could pull back and away if she wanted. She could walk off the dance floor and get a cab home and stop this charade once and for all. But he was tall and strong and his body was hard and compelling against hers and he had a power over her that she could barely understand.

For a moment Jane closed her eyes and let herself be held by him. He didn't wear cologne but she could smell the masculine scent of whatever he'd used in his hair to mess it into his model style. Her face was turned towards him, not far from his neck, and his skin was warm. She could hear, faintly and to a different rhythm from the song, the whoosh of his heartbeat and the swish of his breathing.

A step backwards, one to the side. Her hip was between his legs, his thigh between hers, so close they brushed with every movement. Even through clothes, it was intimate. The way their bodies fitted together, moved together. His leg wasn't quite touching her crotch, but his steps shifted the silk of her dress, sent a rustle and a vibration up her body that she felt as definitely as if he had slid a hand underneath her clothes to stroke her.

Days ago, they'd been this close. She'd taken off her underwear for him. He'd slipped his hands up over her bare legs under her dress and given her mind-blowing pleasure. And then touched her with his mouth.

Jane shuddered slightly.

If he did it again, she would react the same way. She would be putty in his hands, shaking in the grip of the orgasm he gave her.

He'd felt her shudder. She heard him make a low sound in his throat, and he brought their linked hands even closer to rest on his chest, pulling her more snugly against him. Her belly flattened against his.

The song stopped and he held her still, a moment out of time where she could only hear them breathing together, and then the music started again, hazier and dreamlike. Their movements together were so slow that Jane was aware of every exaggerated sway of her hip, the small rubbing of his chest on her breasts. A public form of foreplay, a clothed imitation of the most exquisite lovemaking.

Something she had never done with any other man. Couldn't imagine doing with any other man.

She felt Jonny bury his face in her hair, and inhale a deep breath that pulled her even tighter. 'Jane,' he whispered, so quietly she wasn't even sure that she heard it, and he pressed a kiss into her hair. He shifted his head and kissed her forehead, then the top of her closed eyelid. The slight moisture and heat his lips left behind dissolved into coolness.

Slowly, he unlinked his hand from hers and spread her fingers on his chest. With his now-free hand he smoothed back her hair. Her eyes closed, Jane could feel his fingers sifting through her curls. It was as if every strand had a nerve ending of its own.

His hand settled on her neck, stroked gently around it to her chin, all in time with the hazy music. He tilted up her chin and Jane lifted her head towards him, his breath on her skin, without opening her eyes knowing his mouth was close to her.

If she opened her eyes she'd see how this wasn't real. She'd see his coolness, remember this was all a show. Even without looking she couldn't believe this was real. But she could pretend it was an erotic, wonderful dream.

Jane kept her eyes closed and when he touched his lips to her temple she hitched in a breath, heat rushing through her body. He kissed her cheekbone, down the side of her face, to the hollow underneath her ear where the skin was so sensitive that she felt goose-bumps raise themselves on her arms despite the warmth. A careful, thorough line of kisses along her jaw as she slanted her head to allow him access. And then she felt his mouth on her neck.

His tongue touched the spot where her pulse thrummed, and Jane let out a moan, so low it could have been part of the music. But he felt it, because his kisses, still slow, became more fervent, even more thorough.

Moving of their own accord, Jane's fingers dug into Jonny's shirt, stroking the hard planes of his chest. His heartbeat was faster than the music, now. When Jonny's teeth nipped softly at her neck, she moaned again and her hips, still swaying, ground themselves into his.

She could feel his erection. With every move, every kiss, it rubbed against her. She was so close she could tell his dimensions, compare them with her memories of him hard and hot in her hand. Of him parting her and thrusting inside her as her legs pulled him deeper and she clenched around him.

She moved her hand inches to the side, slipped a fingertip between the buttons of his shirt. His skin nearly burned her. Even through layers of clothing she felt his penis jerk against her and harden even more.

He groaned low and rough. His hand on her waist slid down to cup her buttock and hold her even more intimately against him. A shift of clothing and of pose and he could be inside her again, once again only the two of them in the entire universe.

Pure instinct made her move her head and meet his lips with her own.

Right away their tongues touched and he slipped inside her. Jonny, so real he filled every single one of her senses and made her desperate with wanting. Jonny, whom she'd had so deep inside her body that they had felt like one person, while he'd smiled into her eyes. His lips he used for talking and laughing, his teeth smooth and perfect, that confident, kind smile. His tongue giving her pleasure with his kiss. And their bodies dancing together now with no conscious thought, just harmony.

He parted from her only to kiss her again. And again. The music and his hardness and softness. She wanted all of him and yet his kiss was satisfying in itself, an infinite variety of movement, textures, desire.

The song ended. She only knew it because her heartbeat sounded suddenly louder and she was more aware of his ragged breathing. Again they were caught in time in the pause of the music, and Jonny stilled his mouth on hers, just held her there as if they could stay there for ever.

A drum roll and the music began again, this time with a flourish of clarinet. Something fast and catchy.

Jonny lifted his mouth, kissed her once, softly, on her upper lip, and then the kiss was over. Jane opened her eyes.

His face wasn't cold any more. Instead his eyes were dark blue, pupils dilated with desire, his mouth parted and smeared slightly with her lipstick. She ran her thumb over his lips to remove it, and he just caught the tip of her thumb with his teeth in a gentle, erotic bite.

'Let's get out of here,' Jane said to him. Her voice was husky in her own ears.

She saw him swallow. 'Yes, I need to,' he said, and he shifted her so he held her beside him with his arm around her shoulders pulling her tight. She missed the full-body contact, the sensation of his arousal so near to her. But they were leaving, together, and that idea held so much promise that she barely noticed the sea of people they walked through, the flashing of cameras and sequins, the words she responded to automatically because nothing counted but to get alone with Jonny and feel more of him.

There was a cab waiting outside. He helped her into it, his hand lingering on her hip. When he slid in beside her she nestled against his side again and he held her there.

The lights of London were nothing. Jonny was breathing beside her. She thought about closing the door to her flat behind both of them and pushing his jacket off his shoulders. Kissing him and kissing him. About him lifting her into his arms and walking with her to her bedroom. His bare thigh between hers, his firm belly. She had never seen him completely naked.

Jane bit her lip. Again she couldn't look at him, because if she did she would sob with lust. Instead she watched the lights go by in a blur and recognised her neighbourhood only because her body heated still more, knowing there wasn't much time left before the two of them could be in each other's arms again.

He opened the door for her and helped her out of the cab. She stood, throbbing with desperation, as he paid the driver. Her hands shook as she unlocked the building door and climbed the flight of stairs, Jonny half a step behind her, warming her back with his gaze, even his footfalls masculine enough to build her desperation.

Her flat was a million miles away. He wasn't touching her but she felt every breath he took. At last she slid the key into the lock, twisted the knob, and opened the door.

When she turned to Jonny he was standing with his hands in his pockets.

'We did well, I think,' he said, and the roughness that had been in his voice was smoothed out. 'I think we convinced people, don't you?'

She was awash with desire. She was full of fantasies and emotion. And here was Jonny, her friend Jonny, standing here as if the last half an hour had been erased.

'Convinced people?' she repeated stupidly.

He nodded. 'I'm sure nobody would ever suspect that there's nothing between us.' He pulled one hand out of his pocket and checked his watch. 'And we were out of the party early, too, and in such a way that Thom's unlikely to give me a hard time. I'll have a good few hours to put in on the book before I go to bed.'

Jane sagged against the door. Dignity should have made her keep her mouth shut, but she couldn't help the next words coming out. 'It was all an act? All of it?'

Jonny shrugged. 'It was your idea.' He bent forward, as if to kiss her on the cheek, but then straightened without touching her. 'Goodnight, Jane.'

She watched him go. He had never looked so much like a stranger in a photograph.

CHAPTER ELEVEN

Troubleshooting HTML, part one

If your code doesn't execute as you planned, don't despair. Chances are, your mistake is simple and small, and you'll be able to fix it by manipulating just a bit of your code, rather than trashing the entire thing and starting from scratch.

Unfortunately, relationships are not like this.

JONNY leaned back in his chair, rubbed his eyes beneath his glasses, and stared at the ceiling of his hotel room.

Computers were easier. Computers did what you told them to. If something went wrong with a computer there was always a logical reason for it.

'Please tell me that's not why I've chosen to spend so much time with computers,' he said aloud to the empty room. 'Because that is just sad.'

The room didn't answer. Nor did his laptop. He didn't think he'd find many answers if he did an internet search, either.

Jonny sighed, and got up to stretch his aching back. He had a lot of this book to write, and a screaming deadline that he had to meet if he wanted to get paid, no matter what a mess his personal life was in.

But HTML couldn't keep hold of his attention when all he could think about was Jane in his arms on the dance floor, her skin under his lips and her body sweetly pressing into him.

And then Jane at the door of her flat, with confusion, desire and pain in her grey eyes as he'd served up a little slice of revenge that had tasted bitter in his mouth as soon as he'd said it.

Jonny flung himself back in his chair and pulled up his email application. He opened a blank message, addressed it to Jane, and typed faster than he'd managed all night.

Jane,
It wasn't an act. None of it was an act at all. I'm so in love with you I can't think straight and the only way I can stop myself from falling so much more in love with you that I'll never escape again is to pretend to you that I don't love you, even when I'm showing everybody else that I do.

He stared at the words on the screen.

How could he fix this mess? Was there some little action he could go back and change? The original email he'd sent, their meeting at lunch, the inadvertent cyber-sex session? The exhilarating moments when they'd been joined physically, closer than he'd felt to anyone before?

Even when he'd been making love with her, when it had seemed perfect and wonderful and his dreams come true, it had been going wrong.

His finger hovered over the mouse button to send the email to Jane. After all the deception and the misunderstandings, was the truth going to make anything any better?

Jonny pictured her sitting in that bare flat, at her desk, reading his email. He saw her biting her lip and her expressive eyes filling with worry.

She wanted him. But it was because of how he looked, and despite how she felt. And if she didn't love him back, there was no point opening up his heart, because that wasn't going to be fixed easily, either.

He deleted the email, unsent, and clicked back on his word-processing program. He had a lot of work to do, and he certainly wasn't going to get any sleep.

They were in a tree, dangling their legs, except they were all grown up. She wore her silk dress and Jonny's shirt was half open, unbuttoned at the top, his blue tie pulled askew. His hair was tousled but it wasn't from styling. It was from her fingers.

Her mouth felt raw from kissing. Her body was on fire. Jonny took off his glasses and his eyes were bluer than the sky surrounding them.

'Tell me your fantasy,' she said to him. A puff of breeze caught her hair, blew through her bare toes, and made her feel as if she could fly.

'It's you,' he said, and he reached for her.

He touched her and there was music. Hazy and compelling as a heartbeat, filtering through the leaves. Jane slid forward on her branch so she was close to him, close enough to dance. She raised her face to his and kissed him one more time.

And then they were falling down, and the limbs of the tree were hitting the ground before them, hitting with dull thuds.

Just before they reached the ground Jane sat up straight in bed, her heart racing and her body barely able to believe that she wasn't falling through space, and she wasn't in Jonny's arms.

'Stupid dream,' she muttered, pushing her hair back from her face. It was tangled and damp with sweat. She kicked aside the covers and swung her legs out of bed and she heard the dull thuds from her dream again.

It was the door. 'Just a minute,' she called, and found a pair of pyjama bottoms on her bedroom chair. The first time she put them on backwards so she had to sit on her bed and put them on again.

Whoever it was was knocking on the door for the third time by the time she finally got to it. When she opened it, it was Jonny.

He had on jeans and a zip-up sweatshirt and his dark-rimmed glasses and despite all this he looked so much as he had in her dream that she couldn't do anything but stare at him in surprise.

'Sleeping in?'

His voice was cheerful, a complete contrast to how he'd left her last night, or the low passionate tones of her dream. He held out a cardboard cup with a plastic lid to her.

'Skinny latte with chocolate. It should wake you up.'

Jane didn't take it. Instead she attempted to push back her hair again, but it was too much of a rat's nest. That should teach her to use hairspray.

'Why are you here?' she asked.

'Bringing you your favourite coffee?' He held it closer to her. 'Why else?'

'We've got a date, remember?'

She frowned, thinking back. 'No. I don't remember.'

'We're going away for the weekend.'

Comprehension dawned. 'You mean, what you told Gary and Kathleen? But that was a lie, right?'

'Nope.' He nudged a suitcase on the floor with his foot. 'We've got a train in forty-five minutes.'

'Why?'

Jonny shook his head. 'Take the coffee, and let me in, and I'll pretend I'm not insulted by your being so appalled that I want to go away with you for the weekend.'

She took the coffee and stood back to let him in. He picked up his bag and another cup of coffee from the floor and strode inside. Jane tried not to think about how awful she looked.

'I'm not appalled,' she said. 'I'm just surprised. I thought you'd made up that date on the spur of the moment to annoy Gary. Which worked spectacularly, by the way, and thank you.'

'I did. But the more I thought about it, the more I realised it would be a good idea for us to actually go away.'

Really go away somewhere romantic with Jonny? Jane thought about spending the entire weekend close enough to touch him without being able to, and she was simultaneously filled with longing and despair.

She shook her head a bit to clear it of memories and the traces of her dream, which seemed to be hovering around the corners of her mind. It didn't work.

'Why? Do you think Gary will actually try to check up on us?'

'You're the one who knows him best,' Jonny said. He didn't sound very pleased about the fact. Jane decided it was superfluous to tell him she couldn't possibly know Gary very well, if she'd never suspected him cheating on her until it had been rubbed in her face.

'I can always just not answer my phone,' she said instead.

'Not good enough. It's safer if we get out of London.' He sa
down at her desk and turned on her laptop. 'Have you done a
software update on this lately?'

'What? No.'

He glanced down at the baseboard. 'Wireless broadband, excellent. There'll be enough time for me to do a quick update
while you go get showered and packed. I'm guessing your RAM
needs defragging, too.'

'Jonny, I don't need you to—'

His smile was so sudden and so warm that she couldn't continue

'Jane, let me update your computer. I'm good at it, and I'll
enjoy doing it for you. And let me take you away for the weekend
I'm hoping I'll be good at that, too.'

'But *why* do you want to go away with me?' she asked,
finally, in desperation, feeling as she had in her dream, falling
off the tree.

'I want to start again,' he said. 'I feel like we've messed all of
this up, somehow, and I want to forget about this act we're putting
on and just be you and me for a little while. It's the same thing
you asked me last night on the balcony. Only for longer.'

'You want to go away as friends,' Jane said. Again, she had
the odd feeling of two opposite emotions warring for supremacy.
This time it was both relief and disappointment, and the combination made her stomach do a distinct roll, as if it couldn't decide
which way to go.

'Sure,' he said, smiling. 'Go and get ready.'

In the absence of any clear-cut response, she went towards her
bedroom to follow Jonny's request. Near the door, she stopped
and turned around.

'You're trying to save money,' she said. 'I can't let you pay
to take me away for the weekend.'

'Okay,' he said, already typing away on her laptop. 'You can
pay for your train ticket. I won't let it bother my manly pride.'

Jane stood in the door, considering Jonathan Cole, her childhood friend, whom, apparently, she was going to spend a totally
platonic weekend with.

And wondered how she could be so turned on by somebody fixing her computer and talking about his lack of manly pride.

Jane peeped up over the screen of her laptop. Across the train table, Jonny was bent over his own keyboard, his eyes behind his glasses intent. Every line of his body and face appeared totally focused on what he was doing; she could hear his fingers flying over the keyboard.

She'd made it a condition of their trip that she would be able to do some work. There was a meeting with Giovanni Franco and his team on Monday afternoon, where the team would present the mock-ups of the campaign using some of the photographs of Jonny and, though everything was going smoothly, with Franco's reputation as a tricky client she wanted to make sure the presentation was extra-carefully put together, especially as neither Allen Pearce nor Michael Grey, the agency's partners, could be there because they were both at a conference in New York.

Jonny had shrugged and smiled in that easygoing way she'd seen so little of the night before. 'Fine with me, I've got a book to finish,' he'd said. So as soon as they'd boarded the train at Euston they'd both broken out their laptops and sat across from each other at the table, working the entire time.

Well, at least she'd pretended to be working the entire time. Jonny was distracting. Not that he was doing anything, aside from getting them coffee every now and then. He'd tried to talk with her once or twice, but she'd pretended to be too involved in what she was doing to reply.

But his knees weren't far from hers underneath the table. Every once in a while he rested his left hand on the table next to his laptop, and, though it was pathetic, the sight of his hand not even doing anything made her think of him holding her, stroking her back as they danced, giving her pleasure. It tempted her to take his hand and rub it against her cheek, just to learn better how his fingers felt, the knuckles and sinews and strength.

He pushed his glasses up his nose every now and then, too. That shouldn't be sexy, but it was. It was an automatic gesture that made him seem so human, and it made Jane want to push their computers aside and jump across the table and kiss him senseless.

And then, of course, she could smell him. Not an overt scent, just Jonny, in the air she breathed. If Giovanni Franco could bottle his scent as a cologne, they wouldn't need advertising to sell it.

Overall, it was a good thing that she'd insisted on working, even though she wasn't being very efficient. She could only imagine how lust-sodden she'd have been if she hadn't had something to distract her from her friend Jonathan Cole as they sped through the English countryside towards the Lake District.

Her laptop made a soft chime, and she looked down at it in surprise. On the screen was a message:

Twenty minutes till Penrith. Do you think we've worked enough yet? J.

She glanced back up at Jonny, who met her eyes and gave her a cheeky smile and, hell, she didn't just want to throw herself across the table and kiss him—she wanted to throw herself across the table and grab the front of his sweatshirt and drag him off to the cramped and no doubt disgusting train toilet and have wild and frantic sex with him.

I've just got to finish this slide show.

After typing that she vowed to keep her attention on the screen for the next twenty minutes.

Well, at least he knew why Jane was so successful at her job. For the entire three hours and twenty-six minutes of their journey she had beavered away on her laptop, and every time he'd tried to catch her eye or start a conversation she'd appeared to be completely absorbed in what she was doing. A couple of times he'd caught her glancing in his direction, but immediately she was looking back at her computer as if it had never happened.

His own concentration wasn't so good. He'd typed plenty, but he was pretty sure it was gibberish. He'd managed maybe an hour

f solid work, but then he'd gone to get them a coffee and noticed
ow Jane studiously avoided any eye contact or any appearance
f even noticing him, and it occurred to him that her dedication
o work was just a little extreme. Extreme enough to be inter-
reted as trying to avoid talking with him.

Sitting across from her was a pleasure in itself. He could
nagine the two of them working together, stopping to share a
mile, exchange thoughts and solve problems together. It could
e that way once they had recovered the ease between them.
Vhich, of course, might never happen.

Jonny pushed up his glasses, shut down his laptop, and folded
t up as he recognised the long curve approaching Penrith station.
f she wanted to work, that was fine. If she wanted to avoid
alking to him, that was less fine, but he could handle it. He had
er for the entire weekend, after all, and she wasn't going to be
ble to avoid him for ever.

Meanwhile, he would be as friendly as he could be. Jane
vaited until the very last minute to shut down her own laptop and
ack it away.

'Get a lot done?' he asked her.

She shrugged. 'There's still a lot to do. Giovanni Franco's
eam like to have absolutely every "t" crossed and "i" dotted.'

'Sounds like a lot of work. Is it worth it?'

'The contract is one of the most prestigious going right now.'

'I meant, is it worth it to you? It's a Saturday, after all.'

Jane's eyes were expressive enough so that he could tell that
he had no idea what he was talking about. 'Of course.' She
lipped her laptop into her case. 'You've been hard at work, too.'

'Yes, but I've got to make a lot of money in the shortest time
ossible. Plus, writing is a flexible job. I can take a few days off
o enjoy myself, as long as I make it up another time.'

'My job isn't like that. The team is depending on me to nail the
ontract, and I have to do whatever it takes to make that happen.'

'What about you? Aren't you depending on yourself, too, to
nake yourself happy every once in a while?'

'I'll be happy when this contract is all sewn up.' She reached up
o take down her bag from the overhead rack, but he beat her to it.

'You don't have to do that,' she said.

'When are you going to figure out that I like to do things fo you?' He handed her the bag. 'I wouldn't mind making yo happy, either.'

'Amy tells me you did a wonderful job with the photos. Tha makes me happy.'

She was shut up tighter than a clam, determined not to giv an inch. He tried one more time. 'Is it really only work tha makes you happy?'

Jane smiled at him, a little too bright to be true.

'Well, you haven't told me where we're going, but I'r guessing that since we're in the Lake District we might b visiting your mother. I'll be happy to see her again. It's beer what, fifteen years?'

The train stopped. Jane reached for the button to open th carriage door, but Jonny beat her to it again. They stepped ou onto the platform. The air felt cooler, fresher than in London.

He looked at Jane. Her clothes were pure city: carefull pressed and tailored trousers and blouse, a light woollen jacke shiny leather shoes with a little heel. The only reminder of th girl she'd been was her fine skin with the faint flush on he cheeks, her curly hair, her china-doll eyes and lips. She couldn' hide that. The rest was an image, her professional front, preserve even on a Saturday on holiday.

He thought he'd feel different once he was up here in th Lakes. He'd thought about Jay Richard as a persona he could slij on, walk around in for a while, and then slip off again. He' thought once he got up here, the place that he always thought o as home even though he'd only really lived here for seven or eigh years, he'd be back being Jonny Cole, somebody comfortabl and cheerful and straightforward, who didn't care about appear ances or particularly what other people thought about him.

But he didn't feel different. When he was Jay, he still had al the emotions and the attitude of Jonny. And now that he wa Jonny, he was still thinking about appearances and what they saic about a person.

For example, whether Jane's nearly aggressive professional

ism was just a front to hide her real self, or if it had, over the years, become her real self.

'Jonny?' Jane said, and he realised he'd been standing on the platform, staring at her, lost in his thoughts. 'Are you okay?'

'Yeah. I was wondering if masquerading as Jay Richard had given me anything worthwhile except a knowledge of how to use hair gel.'

She laughed, though not wholeheartedly, still acting as awkward as she'd been all day. 'It's made you some money, at least.'

He nodded. 'And given me an excuse to kiss you every now and then.'

She flushed, and looked away from him, down the platform. 'Where are we going now?'

'Lunch,' he said decisively, and touched her arm to guide her down the platform. It was unnecessary, but he'd just sat across from her for three and a half hours without touching her and he was only human, after all.

'Lunch, and the truth,' he added. He'd waited a while for that, too.

Jane looked both startled and anxious, but she didn't say anything, just walked with him through the station to where he'd parked his car when Thom had come to get him on Tuesday morning. He loaded their bags into the boot and drove them into Penrith proper, to one of the cafés in the town centre that catered to both tourist and local trade. It wasn't high season yet, so aside from two or three full tables they had the place largely to themselves.

'What do you mean, the truth?' Jane asked, once they were settled at a table, menus in front of them.

She looked uncomfortable enough that he instinctively smiled at her. 'Order lunch first,' he said, noticing a waitress was approaching. 'You might be able to live on work and air, but I need food.'

They ordered their lunch and Jane folded her hands on the table. Jonny remembered the first time they'd sat across the table with each other. She'd twisted a strand of her hair around her finger, each small turn of her finger another lure to his heart.

'The truth is,' he said, 'I've lured you up here under false pretences.'

'I'm still not quite sure what your pretences were in the first place.'

'I don't just want to be your friend.'

Jane's fingers clenched on each other, and she bit her lip. 'Jonny, we've already talked about—'

'No, we haven't,' he interrupted. 'You've told me that you don't want to have a relationship with me because you don't want to lose me as a friend. I haven't told you what I want, and how I feel about it.'

'Okay,' she said, and he could tell she was steeling herself for something. 'What do you want, and how do you feel about it?'

'I want you,' he said.

She instantly flushed, from her delicate collar-bone to the roots of her hair, and it was all Jonny could do not to reach out and put his hand on her skin to feel the heat.

'From the minute I saw you I wanted to touch you. I'm so attracted to you that I described to you how I wanted to make love with you. And that fantasy wasn't an all-purpose fantasy. It was about *you,* Jane. The reason I could tell it to you was because I haven't felt quite this way about anybody else.'

'Jonny, I don't think it's a good idea—'

'No, I know you don't. I also happen to know that you're attracted to me, too. Let's face it, Jane, when we had sex it was more than just exciting and good. It was amazing. Absolutely mind-blowing. For both of us. And both of us would like to do it again. You can deny it if you want, but I held you and danced with you and kissed you last night and you wanted me as badly as I wanted you.'

She didn't appear to be able to answer. Her cheeks were even pinker than before.

'When I walked away from you at the door it was one of the most bloody difficult things I've ever done. It actually hurt. Not just because of how turned on I was—which made it distinctly uncomfortable to walk up and down those stairs, let me tell you—but because I knew you were feeling exactly the same way. I also knew that leaving you at your doorstep was a mean, petty little bit of revenge on you for cutting off our sexual relationship before it even began properly. And that knowledge doesn't make me feel great about myself.'

'So you've—' She cleared her throat, and started again. 'So the real reason why you've taken me up here for a weekend away with you is so that we can have sex with each other again?'

Wouldn't he love that? Drive her to Keswick, carry her up the stairs to his flat, into his bedroom, and lose himself in Jane for the entire weekend.

And her eyes were wide and sexy, her breath was coming quickly. He could do it. A little convincing, a kiss like the ones they'd shared on the dance floor. Whispering in her ear what he'd like to do with her.

The attraction between them was enough that Jane would forget all her scruples. She'd been willing to last night.

'No,' he said, and a part of him, the part that was ruled purely by libido, was kicking himself.

'Oh,' she replied. A definite hint of disappointment in her voice.

'Because I don't just want sex with you,' he continued, before his kicking libido and Jane's disappointment made him forget all about logic, reason, and self-preservation.

'I want a relationship. I want us to date and to get to know each other and to care about each other and trust each other. I want something real between us. That's what I was hoping was going to happen when you told me you'd split up with Gary, and you wanted to go out on a date with me. That you and I would become something much more than friends. More even than lovers.'

Her face was a picture of astonishment, so he kept talking, because he didn't feel like being let down.

'But what happened afterwards made that impossible. I'd like a relationship with you, Jane, maybe something serious. But any relationship I have has to be based one hundred per cent on trust and truthfulness. What we've got instead is a pact to deceive people. And for whatever reason, you're doing your best to shut me out of your feelings. So we can't have a relationship. We can't have sex, because that will just make me want much more. All I can hope for is that we can salvage our friendship.'

Jane opened her mouth to say something, but at that moment

their lunch arrived. From the look on her face, Jonny figured she wasn't any hungrier than he was, but she picked up her fork and played with a bit of salad anyway.

'I didn't know you felt that way,' she said at last. 'Not that strongly.'

'Now you do.' He made himself take a bite of his beef and ale pie, because, although he'd just exposed his heart to her, he didn't particularly want to dwell on it or elaborate on it. His libido was kicking him enough without his emotions joining in, too. He'd rather have lunch.

Jane followed suit. The noise of cutlery on crockery seemed less awkward than silence.

He wasn't watching her, but he knew every single bite she took, every light touch of her gaze on his face. After several minutes she put her fork down.

'I do want to be friends with you, Jonny. Real friends.'

As that was the best he was going to get, he made himself smile at her.

'Good. Because that's the other reason I brought you up here. I could use a friend for what I'm going to do next.'

'What's that?'

'You were right about my mother. My father wasn't honest with her, but I have to be. She needs to know about her financial situation and what Dad was up to.'

'It's not going to be easy to tell her,' Jane said softly.

'No. I'm not looking forward to it. It would be good to have you around.'

Jane nodded. 'I'll help out however I can.'

'Being there will be enough. You're the only other person who knows the truth.'

'When do you want to tell her?'

'Probably the sooner the better. We can go straight to Ullswater to the hotel.'

'That's fine.' Her tone was decisive, almost businesslike, but it was also kind and warm.

This time, the smile they shared wasn't forced, and when Jonny went back to his lunch, he realised it tasted good.

* * *

Parkhouse Bay Hotel nestled between trees, set back from the narrow road by a carefully tended garden. The house was constructed of slivers of stacked grey slate. Tall chimneys and windows made it seem even larger.

Jonny turned off the ignition of his car and they sat together. Jonny was looking at the house; Jane was looking at Jonny. His face was thoughtful and sad.

'When we first moved up here we had a little bed and breakfast across the lake,' he said. 'There were only three guest bedrooms and my parents and I squeezed into two rooms total. They risked everything to come up here; my father packed in his job and they took out loans and they worked every hour they could because my mother had always dreamed of running a hotel in the Lakes. When she saw this hotel, she fell in love with it. It was years before it came on the market, but when it did, they were ready.'

He paused, and Jane wondered if she should say something. She wanted to ease his sadness, but she didn't know how.

'I always thought about it as the castle my father built for my mother,' he said. He shot her a quick glance, and she was glad she hadn't said anything after all, just let him have space with his own thoughts. 'He was always so protective of her. Every day when I looked at them I could see how happy they were together. He was my model for everything.'

Her hand lifted to take his, but then she stopped. She wasn't sure if that was what she should do. 'You really had no idea he wasn't what he seemed?'

'None. I wanted to work hard and find a woman to love as much as he loved my mother. I wanted a relationship just like theirs.'

He kept on looking at the house, but Jane could feel how his words were directed at her.

Over lunch, he'd said that he wanted a real relationship with her. Something serious. And this was what he'd meant. Love, protectiveness, marriage, building castles.

Her whole body warmed; the air in the car seemed suddenly stifling. What she felt could be embarrassment, could be pleasure, could be fear. She had an overwhelming urge to roll down the window and gulp air.

'But it was all a lie,' he continued, quietly. 'It's so strange. I can't understand it.'

'I understand it,' Jane said, and she was surprised both by what she'd said and by how Jonny's head snapped around to her, pinning her with his blue eyes.

'I mean, I don't understand it, quite. But I know what it's like. You don't set out for it to be that way. It just grows, without you even noticing, and then one day you realise you don't even know who the other person is. Or who you are.'

She'd been talking about her and Gary, but as soon as she said the last few words she realised she was talking about her and Jonny, too.

It was exactly what he'd said: what was between them wasn't honest.

It was her fault. Gary had been the cheating one, but maybe it had been her fault with him, too. She didn't know how to have a relationship; she'd failed at her engagement and now she was failing with Jonny. It was painful for him to be here, and she was making it even worse for him.

She didn't just want to open the window; she wanted to bolt out of the car and run all the way back to London.

Then Jonny suddenly smiled at her. His sunny smile, digging those lines in his cheeks, making his eyes bright.

'I'm glad you're here with me,' he said to her.

Jane smiled back, but unaccountably she also felt her eyes pricking.

'Me too,' she said. This time she did take his hand, and squeezed it.

She didn't know how to do a relationship—not the kind of relationship he wanted, something built on trust and truth, something that could create love and castles. But she was going to do her damnedest to be his friend.

Even though she wasn't sure she knew how to do that, either.

CHAPTER TWELVE

JONNY spread the last of the papers on the table between him and his mother and, for the first time, really looked across at her.

There was a frown on her forehead, deepening a line between her blue eyes. But her hands were steady, and her lips, though pressed together, were firm.

'Is that all of it?' she asked.

'That's all.' And plenty, he would have thought. The mortgages, the loans, thousands of pounds and no indication of where it should come from.

She nodded. She seemed to be very calm, and that disturbed Jonny more than any crying or shouting would have done. When he was a child, his mother had cried every now and then. A film on television, a hurt animal in the garden, the soap opera on the radio—those things had made her cry and lean into his father's arms for comfort. The tears about trivialities came easily and went easily, too, dissolving into laughter, their only purpose the impetus for an exchange of love.

At her husband's funeral, Naomi Cole hadn't shed a tear. She had stood like a ghost, like half a person, strong and yet desperately reduced.

'It's a lot of money,' she said. 'I didn't know it was so much. Why didn't you tell me?'

'You had enough worries dealing with Dad's death, and keeping the hotel going.'

She met his eyes for the first time, and her look was keen. 'You thought you'd pay it off yourself, didn't you? Is this the reason for the second job with Thom? And the talk about going back to doing some consulting?'

'Yes.'

She nodded again. 'You worked hard to retire from the big company and be your own boss. Then you find out about all these loans and give up your dream.'

'I haven't given up my dream. I'm still writing the books; I'm just doing other things, too.'

'You shouldn't be supporting your mother. You should be establishing yourself so you can start your own family.' Naomi's eyes flickered to the closed door of the kitchen; Jane was sitting in the living room, giving the two of them space to talk.

'That's a long way away,' Jonny said. 'And the hotel isn't going to make enough income to pay these bills.'

'I can sell the hotel.'

'You're not going to sell the hotel,' Jonny said. 'It's the only thing you've got left of Dad.'

That made her frown deepen, and her gaze sharpen. 'I've got more of your father than a building we bought together.'

The financial bad news had been easy, compared to this. What he was going to say next was going to take his mother's faith and crush it. It was going to smash every memory into ashes, leave nothing but the slate and wood of this hotel.

Jonny clenched his hands on the table. 'Mum, I need to tell you about why Dad owes all this money.'

'You mean his gambling?'

In the wedding photos, Jonathan Cole, senior, looked like his son. He didn't have the same striking perfection of features, but there were the same smile lines dug in his cheeks, and the same laughing mouth. He was tall, dark and handsome. In every photo he was touching his new wife: holding her hand, pulling her closer, stealing a kiss. Even in the big, formal photo that was framed in the centre of the living room wall, he had his fingers twined with Naomi's. His body leaned towards her, their eyes locked in an embrace that was more intense than anything physical.

Jane absently bit her fingernail as she wandered along the side of the room, looking at each photograph in turn. There were years of Jonathan and Naomi Cole together, on holiday or at home. Jane recognised the London suburb she'd grown up in. Jonathan had been on the local cricket team, and, even when Naomi wasn't in the pictures, Jane could tell the ones where she had been behind the camera. Even through years and the glass of the photo frames, she could read Jonny's father's love for his wife.

She hadn't known Jonny's parents' story, really, but she could extrapolate it from the photographs. From hairstyles and clothes fashions, it was several years after their wedding when the first photograph of Naomi pregnant appeared. Then baby photos. Jonny had been a chubby lump of a baby, and Jane bet anything he'd campaigned in his adolescence to get those particular photographs locked away out of sight.

She picked up one of him as a skinny and bespectacled child and studied it more closely. This was how she remembered him, but, now that she looked at it, she could see the straight line of his jaw, the full curve of his lip, the innocent cheekbones. Everything that would make him so beautiful when he was an adult was in place, though not yet focused. A whip-thin, angular blur of a child, overwhelmed by thick lenses and the fringe of thick brown hair.

But that smile. That was there, in baby teeth. It had always been there.

Jane put the photograph down and sat in an armchair. Jonny and his mother had been talking for about an hour and a half, while she waited here. The walls that didn't have photos on them were lined with books, there was a television, and she could always do some work. But instead her eyes kept being drawn to the photographs. The documentation of three lives, one family.

Her mother had photographs, too—a pride wall in the living room. There weren't any wedding photos, though; those must have come down after Jane's parents divorced, when she was about six. There was a photograph of her mother in her army officer uniform, and photos of Jane and her brothers winning races, receiving their degrees, accepting honours. Jane had rarely looked at them growing up, nor these days, when she visited her mother. They were invisible as the wallpaper.

Her father, when she saw him, didn't have photographs. He

noticed actions, not pictures. He noticed noise and slaps on the back and job promotions.

She stood again and went back to the pictures on the sideboard, family shots of the three Coles together. These pictures were looked at all the time. Naomi was an hotelier, and a careful housekeeper, but the glass had fingerprints.

They were captured images of warmth and love. They showed the kind of life that Jonny wanted to create over again for himself. They were what he feared had never really been true.

And she hadn't done much for his opinion of relationships, either.

She heard a door open behind her and she turned, quickly putting down the picture of Jonny and his parents. Naomi came in, looking serene as usual, though her blue eyes were perhaps a little pink at the edges. Jonny, on the other hand, was pale and he kept on blinking, as if he were slightly shell-shocked.

The impulse to go and hug him was one of the strongest she'd ever had. However, she wasn't sure whether Naomi even knew she knew what they'd been talking about, so instead she just met his eyes and tried to figure out how he felt, what he needed.

'Jane, you haven't been sitting here for all this time without so much as a cup of tea, have you?' said Naomi, shaking her head as if all she had to worry about was the status of Jane's thirst.

'I'm fine, Mrs Cole,' she said.

'Well, come into the kitchen and I'll make you one. You must be thirsty and I'm afraid I need to put you to work. I've only got a few guests in for an evening meal tonight and when that happens we all eat together.'

She let herself be swept up into the large kitchen and furnished with a cup of tea and some vegetables for peeling. Jane peered around the room, hoping for some sign of what had passed in it, but all of Jonny's folder of papers had been cleared away, and the place was scrupulously tidy, a Victorian kitchen adapted to both domestic and hotel use. No lingering scent of heartbreak in the air.

That didn't mean much, though. Jonny had told her that his mother didn't express her emotions easily. Unlike her son, who, she was beginning to understand, normally wore his emotions honest on his face.

Naomi was discussing pudding with him, giving him a big shopping bag of apples, and, although she could tell this was a task they had shared hundreds of times, she could also tell that Jonny was looking at his mother as if he were seeing her for the first time, despite the familiarity of his words and gestures.

It was between the two of them. She wanted to help.

Instead she picked up a knife and began scraping carrots.

'Jane Miller!' Naomi appeared at her side. 'You can't do that to a carrot. You'll slice your fingers off. Use a peeler.'

'A peeler?'

Again, Naomi appeared to be fully concerned only with Jane. 'Do you cook, dear?'

'Not really,' she admitted. 'I scramble an egg occasionally.'

'Your mother never taught you?'

'My mother always said that the army taught her how to eat anything and cook nothing. She showed us some basics.'

'But you and those brothers of yours were too interested in creating mayhem than learning to cook. She had her hands full with the five of you, I remember. Lucky woman.'

For a moment, Naomi's face did show an unbidden emotion: wistful longing. And Jane knew how this woman whose career revolved around making people feel at home felt about only having the one, precious child after years of trying.

'Right.' Naomi, all efficiency again, took the carrot from Jane's hand and rummaged in a drawer, coming out with some instruments. 'I am going to give you a cookery lesson. And while I do, you can catch me up on how your mother and brothers are doing.'

Jane glanced over at Jonny, who was peeling and coring apples. He had a sure hand with the fruit. Just as he knew how to fix a computer, how to dress, how to write a book, how to put across a perfect appearance even though he didn't care about appearances. And yet something about him seemed uncertain right now—not his movements, not his appearance, just whatever it was that made him Jonny.

She could haul him out of the kitchen and ask him what had

happened, give him the hug she wanted to give him. Somehow, though, she knew that the best thing for her to do was to keep his mother occupied, let herself be mothered and let Jonny come to whatever adjustment he needed to in his own time.

She had no idea how she knew this. She only hoped it was right.

So she learned how to make a chicken and leek pie big enough to feed ten people. She told Naomi about her brothers' lives, how her mother kept busy with the Territorial Army and charity organisations, about her own job and what it was like to live in London. As soon as the pie was in the oven there were potatoes to mash, and a salad to make, and the bustle of setting the big table in the hotel dining room and meeting the guests, all flushed from a day's hill-walking, and Jane didn't have time to say a word to Jonny until she sat down next to him at the table to eat.

And then they were in front of strangers, and there was nothing she could say to find out what had happened. So she slipped her hand underneath the table while the potatoes were being passed and touched Jonny's thigh, firm and solid in his jeans.

He looked at her, their eyes met, and for the first time in her life Jane understood what it meant to communicate without words.

Are you all right?

I'm okay. We'll talk later.

His hand covered hers for a brief instant and squeezed. They were in a bubble of warmth, a moment for two. Jonny leaned towards her, the side of his face brushing the side of hers, and whispered, 'Thank you.'

Then the potatoes came, and the social conversation, and they weren't touching any more. But Jane felt as though they were.

'She knew.'

Jonny threw himself on his couch, which was big and soft and squishy. His face was pale, the cheekbones seeming more pronounced.

'About the debt?'

'About some of the debt. Not all of it. But she knew about my father's gambling.'

Jane joined him on the couch. She'd felt close to him all through dinner, surrounded by people, but then, once they'd actually been alone in his car, she'd started doubting again. He'd driven with concentration down the dark and twisting roads to his flat in Keswick, and every second of silence had seemed like an hour to her. That sudden gift of being able to communicate without words had disappeared.

And now they were alone on his couch and she wasn't quite sure what to say any more. The hug she'd so wanted to give him when they were in his mother's hotel seemed too much to offer and ask, too much like the sexual contact they couldn't have.

'How'd she find out?' she asked, keeping a safe distance from him on the couch. If she got too close, she would smooth back his hair, try to caress colour into his cheeks.

'She's always known. He's been a problem gambler for years. He told her soon after they married, apparently. It used to be the horses, the football, anything he could bet on at the bookies'. She helped him with it, she said, and he went for long stretches without gambling, but sometimes he would slide. Times of stress. She didn't know it then, but she thinks now that maybe finding out about his heart disease scared him back into the old pattern.'

'And you never suspected?'

'Never. They were—they were too close to let such a secret out from between them, even to me.' For the first time, Jonny looked at her, and his eyes were the colour of a wind-tossed lake, a restless sea. 'He must have been very frightened, to go so far.'

His eyes and his words got rid of her inhibitions. Jane slid across the couch and put her arms around Jonny's shoulders and hugged him.

He responded immediately by wrapping his arms around her tight and pulling her to sit on his lap. He buried his face in her hair and Jane felt him breathing deep, nestling in closer to her. Her cheek rested against his neck, where his pulse beat under his skin.

Time reduced to heartbeats and breaths taken, Jonny's scent

and warmth drawn down into her body. She was offering him comfort, she knew, but she had never felt so safe.

An indefinable number of moments later, he loosed one of his arms from around her and stroked his hand through her hair. Long, slow strokes, as if he were soothing her, too, by sifting his fingers through her curls.

She raised her head and did what she'd wanted to earlier. The skin of his face was warm and just rough with stubble, the bones precise and perfect under her hand. With her touch she saw colour come back along with his half a gentle smile.

'Thank you,' he said.

'I didn't do much.'

'You were there. That was what I wanted.'

'How do you feel?'

He blinked a few times, considering, and she noticed that the colour of his eyes had calmed back into deep blue. He had his father's mouth, but his mother's eyes.

'Better,' he said, and sounded surprised. 'My father wasn't the perfect man I thought he was. But he and my mother had a real marriage.'

Still caressing his face, she remembered the photographs. Jonathan and Naomi Cole's real marriage had been a part of every day of Jonny's life. He'd grown up feeling an integral part of his family, wanted and valued not just for who he was and what he did, but because he completed the unit just by existing.

No wonder his flat, which he'd moved into five months before, was already more homelike than any place Jane had ever lived. No wonder he had that warmth in his voice and his smile, that ability to be happy in his honest self and to make her feel special.

He was special himself. He had those gifts she had never been given, that she'd never even known that she lacked.

She hadn't even learned how to be a friend until a few hours ago.

Jonny was still brushing his fingers through her hair. He let his hand rest on her nape, his thumb making slow circles. The touch on her bare skin made her shiver.

Without planning it, she lifted his glasses off and put them aside on the arm of the couch. He didn't look that different without them. The same, just more…naked.

As if she'd begun to undress him.

She traced, with a finger, one of his eyebrows. It was soft and glossy. She followed the curve of it downward and then, when he shut his eyes, brushed the skin of his eyelid. Still soothing, still gentle. The skin here seemed somehow exposed, more delicate and sensitive than normal skin. Hot, protecting the precious eye beneath. It reminded her of the smooth skin on his erection, the one time she had held him in her hands and heard him gasp with pleasure.

Only that one time. Only for a moment. Not nearly enough.

She moved her head, lifted and tilted so she could press her lips to that delicate skin. Under her lips she felt the small movement of his eye, and she heard the soft exhalation of his breath.

Touching him was addictive. She kissed the ridge of his eye socket, his forehead, loving how she could feel the bones under his skin. With her lips she could appreciate the texture of his eyebrows. She pushed back his hair and kissed where it began to grow from his head, the roots tickling her.

Jonny's arms tightened around her. The way she was sitting meant that her right breast was pressed against his chest, and his heartbeat went through her. It was a small rhythmic caress on her stiffened nipple. He slid his hand around her neck, running his thumb now along the side of her jaw, his other hand spread across the small of her back.

His touch was still comforting, but Jane drew in a breath full of him, heard their clothes rustling in the silence and the soft kisses of her lips, and knew that they had gone from soothing each other to arousing. His legs under hers were hard and she could feel his erection, even harder, underneath one of the cheeks of her bottom. He surrounded her and held her and she couldn't resist touching the skin of his forehead once, just briefly, with her tongue to taste faint salt and Jonny.

She had never yet lain down with him, naked, skin to skin. She wondered whether he would feel like this, comfortable and yet exciting.

'Jane,' Jonny whispered.

She was under a spell woven by his body under hers and their closeness and she knew that he had whispered because he couldn't bear to break it either. 'Mmm,' she answered, kissing his cheekbone, the slight hollow underneath it. The line his smile created.

'We agreed not to do this,' he whispered.

'I know.' She kissed the line beside his mouth again. If she moved slightly to the left, she could kiss his mouth. She knew what it would be like. The hesitation would be gone and she would need to devour his lips, slide her tongue into his mouth and feel everything about him.

Or she could shift her head slightly upwards, and look into his eyes. She knew what that would be like, too. It would be reality returning, and the rational agreement they'd made not to have sex with each other. Because she couldn't give him what he needed.

Instead she kissed him a third time. He was slightly sandpapery with a day's growth and when he smiled there would be a groove. Just there, where her lips parted. But he wasn't smiling now because he wanted her and it was wrong.

The corner of his mouth. So close to a real kiss. She could make him turn to her and kiss her as she wanted him to. She could run her hand down his chest and touch the bulge in his jeans, unzip his flies and take him out and drive them both out of control.

She moved her hand down his chest. He was breathing even more quickly. His belt buckle was cool. She touched the tip of her tongue to the corner of his mouth.

'Jane,' he groaned, louder now, and anyone listening would think he was encouraging her to touch him.

But he wasn't moving. He was waiting, tense, for what she was going to do. Eaten up with anticipation, but not moving.

Because she wasn't what he really wanted.

Jane bit her lip. Then she bowed her head and quickly, before she could change her mind, she slipped off his lap and to her feet.

'I should go to bed before I do something stupid,' she said. She felt the hated flush creeping up her cheeks.

Jonny stood, too. She couldn't meet his eyes but she could see the grace in his body, and the way his penis strained against his jeans, outlining a shape that fired her memory and imagination.

He touched her cheek and then took his hand away, as if he didn't trust himself any more than she trusted herself. 'Thank you,' he said.

She nodded, not looking at his face. 'No problem. I'm happy to help. Any time you want me to fail to seduce you, just let me know.'

'You haven't failed, believe me. But thank you for stopping. It's better this way.'

She nodded again. 'I know.'

'I'm glad one of us was strong enough to stop it.' She heard him pull in a long breath and let it out. She didn't feel strong. Foolish and inadequate, yes.

'Okay, well, I'll go to bed,' she said. She turned, straightening her blouse, heading for the guest room where Jonny had put her bag earlier.

'Jane.' His voice stopped her, though she wasn't brave enough to turn back to him. 'I also meant thank you for listening. And for telling me I should tell my mother the truth. It was the best thing I could have done.'

'I'm glad.'

She felt his hand tugging at hers, turning her around to face him. She finally looked up into his face and saw his smile and his eyes, so warm with affection. He bent and kissed her on her forehead.

'Let's have a proper break tomorrow,' he said. 'Just you and me, not worrying about anything.'

'As friends.'

'As friends.' His face was kind, and she'd never known that kindness could hurt. 'You told me the other day you didn't know how to be friends. But you do, Jane. You're very good at it.' He squeezed her hand, and then let it go. 'Sleep well.'

She nodded, yet again, too full of thwarted desire and disappointment and embarrassment to do anything else but murmur 'good-night' and go to the guest room, where she knew she would lie awake and think about friendship as if it were a consolation prize.

CHAPTER THIRTEEN

'Now this is what I call a day off.'

Jane made a sound of assent, still gazing down the slope to where Ullswater lay mirror-calm, reflecting the blue spring sky and the crenulated mountains, rich with last summer's bracken and this year's gorse. A dry stone wall was cool behind her back and the spring sun was warm on her face. And Jonny was beside her, strong and tall, sitting on the same blanket among the remains of their picnic, with his back leaning against the same stone wall.

She absently took another grape from the bunch in her lap and popped it in her mouth. The sweetness that exploded on her tongue seemed a part of the view, the smell of new grass, the sound of sheep rustling behind the wall and Jonny's breathing.

They'd spent the morning walking around the lake—nothing too strenuous, because she didn't have proper boots, just trainers, but enough so that her legs felt pleasantly achy and her lungs felt full of fresh air. She realised something.

'I haven't thought about work all day,' she said. Her mobile phone, which would normally be attached to her body in some way, lay turned off in her handbag on Jonny's guest-room bed, next to her BlackBerry. It had felt like a dizzying risk when she had turned their power off. Maybe it was the fresh air, but it felt less risky now.

Jonny laughed. 'I should think not. I can't think of anything more different from that office of yours.' He took one of her grapes. 'I used to come up here when I was in secondary school and I was having a hard time. I'd just sit and look at the lake. It's simpler. Everything is as it seems.'

'I don't think I've gone for a whole morning and afternoon without thinking about work for…' She frowned, and considered. 'I don't think I ever have.'

'You're joking,' Jonny said, and then he obviously looked at her face. 'You're not joking.'

He sounded appalled. 'It's not so strange,' she said. 'You work hard, too.'

'Yes. And when I was in Silicon Valley working for CaliSoft, I took all the fourteen-hour days they could throw at me, and I loved it because I was solving problems. I would go home and write code in my dreams while I was sleeping. There were a couple months when I wouldn't have spoken to a live person face to face if Thom hadn't physically dragged me out to the beach.'

She glanced at Jonny. Before she'd met him again she'd been sure his life was exactly like that—days and nights spent bent over a computer. In real life he was so vital that she couldn't quite imagine him shutting himself away.

'I wrote my first book proposal when I realised I couldn't spend my life in a corporation, letting my time belong to someone else,' he said.

'But you still have to spend hours on your books.'

'Yes. But the great thing about being your own boss, more or less, is that if you work hard enough one day, you can play the next.' He smiled at her ruefully. 'I haven't had much inclination to play since moving back to England, though.'

'I'm not sure I ever have.'

'You must. Surely you don't work every weekend, Jane?'

'Yes. Not always in the office,' she added quickly. 'Sometimes at home.'

'Even when you were with Gary?'

'Gary wanted to work, too.'

But now she wondered whether she hadn't used work to avoid intimacy with Gary, because she knew she wasn't any good at it. And whether he'd only been pretending to want to work, too. He certainly wouldn't be doing much working in the company of Kathleen.

Jonny was shaking his head. 'When you were a kid you used

to play all the time. Every time I came round to your house you and your brothers had concocted some new elaborate game.'

She sighed. 'Those weren't games; they were convoluted tests to make the only girl in the family jump through every hoop to prove she was worthy of not being left behind.'

'Really? I was always jealous of all the fun you had.'

'You're an only child. I love my four brothers, but there was competition for everything. Who was the fastest, the smartest, the cheekiest, who was Mum's favourite, who got invited to spend time with Dad. It was fun sometimes; sometimes it was pure hell.' She stood up, and threw a grape with quick accuracy at a tree trunk. It hit it square on. 'I did learn how to bowl a cricket ball, though.'

Jonny stood, too. 'You learned more than that. Come on.'

He grabbed her hand and tugged her down the slope. Jane let out a giggle of surprise and delight as they ran, avoiding rocks and tufts of grass and small cairns of sheep dung. Her body moved without needing her to think and she remembered flying down a street in Chelsea, also holding Jonny's hand.

He stopped them in front of a tree; not the slim one she'd hit with the bowled grape, but a grandfather of a tree, thick-trunked and tall with gnarled, strong branches. Its young leaves were bright green.

'I bet the view's even better from up there,' Jonny said, pointing to a branch far above their heads.

'You're joking.'

'I'm not.'

'I haven't climbed a tree in—'

'Way too long. Me neither. Let's do it.'

Jonny grinned at her, the sunlight dancing in his eyes, the breeze ruffling his hair. Pure fun.

'All right, Tarzan,' she said, and began to scan the trunk for hand- and footholds. Bole and branches transformed into a ladder. She put her hand on the trunk and fitted her toes into a hole. The bark was rough under her hands, cool and alive.

'Want a boost up?' Jonny asked. She glanced over her shoulder at him and, unbelievably, winked.

'What do you think I am, some sort of girl?' she asked, and hoisted herself upwards.

It was a dozen years, at least, since she'd climbed a tree, but the rhythm and the balance came back to her immediately. She stretched, reached, scrambled, swung. Everything disappeared but the next branch, and the next, until she hauled herself onto the thick branch that Jonny had pointed to, and straddled it.

From here the view was panoramic: the lake, the mountains, even trees beneath her. The leaves were young enough not to block the view, but instead frame it with slivers of green life. Her breath was coming quickly, her heart was thrumming, and she laughed out loud with joy as she swung her feet in the air.

'Is it that good?' Jonny called to her from the ground. From this height he was foreshortened, all head and shoulders.

'Better,' she said.

Jonny began to climb. From her perch she watched him. He took a slightly different route than she had, because he was taller and stronger. She smiled, appreciating the strength of his hands and shoulders, the dexterity of his movements. It took him very little time to reach the branch where she sat. She scooted aside, closer to the trunk, so he could join her.

Like her, he was flushed and excited by his exertion and the height. He sat with his legs dangling off the side and pounded on his chest. 'Ahhhh-ahahhh-ahahhhhhh!' he Tarzan-yelled to the view. His voice came faintly back to them.

Jonny's expression was so self-satisfied that Jane laughed and he laughed with her. She rested her head back against the trunk and for the space of several lung-expanding breaths she was simply happy.

'Penny for them,' Jonny said, after a little while.

For a second she nearly told him about the dream she'd had, about the two of them in a tree, about how he'd said she was his fantasy.

'I was thinking I should do this more often, and wondering if I'd get arrested for climbing a tree in Hyde Park.'

'Before I met you again, that was exactly what I'd have expected you to do,' Jonny said.

Her lips twisted at the implications of that. 'But when you met me again, you realised I wasn't that type of person any more.'

'Not exactly. You did act out one of my most amazing fantasies on the very first night.'

'That was—uncharacteristic.'

'Was it?'

Being up here seemed to get rid of her embarrassment, her reticence. It was as if by climbing up high, she'd left behind the rest of the world and it was just her and Jonny safely cradled in the tree.

'I used to take risks,' she told him. 'It was one of the reasons I was so attracted to the creative side of advertising. I could come up with wild ideas, hundreds of them, ones that nobody else could think of, and sometimes they would stick.'

'Has that changed?'

'Yes. I'm not sure when, exactly. When I started to get promotions, it seemed to be less about coming up with ideas than coming up with the right idea. The one that would sell. Making a success of it. I've got people depending on me now, and it's harder to go out on a limb.' She realised the aptness of the metaphor she'd chosen, and laughed again.

'You were always the most exciting person I knew,' Jonny said. 'You were exactly what I thought every girl should be like.'

'Was,' she said, quietly, glancing away. 'I'm not like that any more.'

A dark bird alighted on the surface of the lake, spreading ripples. She was too far to see what it was, but she watched it paddle, search, and dive.

'Can I ask you a favour?' asked Jonny.

'Of course.'

'You've made one of my fantasies come true lately. I wonder if you would mind helping me with another.'

She looked away from the ripples the bird left on the empty lake and back at Jonny's face. He was serious, but there was still a hint of a gentle smile.

No fear up here, safe from falling. 'All right,' she said.

'I remember sitting up in a tree with you that last time, when nobody knew where we were. You were just like this, leaning against the trunk and laughing. I had the biggest crush on you, Jane. And I couldn't ask you, but all I wanted to do was to kiss you.' He didn't move closer, but the intensity in his eyes was enough to make her feel as if he had. 'Could I kiss you now?'

'Yes,' she said, on a thrill of anticipation. Not even thinking, not even remembering that it was what she'd nearly killed herself to avoid the night before, until she'd agreed.

Jonny swung himself around so he was straddling the branch, too, facing her. He boosted himself along the branch, nearer to her, until their knees touched and their shoes nudged against each other. Then he leaned forward, and she leaned forward at the same time, and their lips met.

She'd kissed Jonny enough so that she should know all about it by now. But while this was familiar, it was new. They touched at their knees and their toes and their mouths, where Jonny was soft and so tender that she had to hold onto the tree branch to keep herself from falling off.

A gentle kiss. A slow kiss. An innocent kiss, in this lofty world with only the two of them. A kiss that ended and then started again, as sweetly as before. A kiss that felt like a first kiss. The fantasy first kiss that she was sharing with Jonny, after all these years.

When he parted from her, she saw her own smile reflected on his face. 'I'm glad we had these days together,' he said.

'Me too.'

He didn't drop her gaze. 'I have this awful suspicion that if I look at my watch I'm going to see that it's time for us to head back so you can get your train.'

Even though her head was nicely spinning, she caught the significance of his pronoun choice. 'You're not coming back to London?'

'The shoot is over, and I have a book to write.'

She bit her lip, tasted Jonny, and understood why their kiss, sweet as it had been, had held a trace of sadness. 'Back to the real world.' The risk of the next three words was easier to take. 'I'll miss you.'

He nodded. 'There's always the computer.'

'Of course.' She took a last breath of Jonny and this special air, and swung both her legs over the same side of the branch. 'Let's go,' she said, and began to climb back down to the real world.

Jane piled her hair up on top of her head and stuck a pencil through it to keep it in place. She glanced at the clock on the wall; it was nearly ten o'clock.

Surely you don't work every weekend, Jane?

She smiled at the memory of Jonny's voice this past afternoon. 'I'm working now because you made me play earlier,' she said aloud. Not to him, because he wasn't here. He was up in his comfortable flat in Keswick, no doubt working too. Or maybe he was at the hotel with Naomi. Whatever he was doing, he was incommunicado, because she had her laptop open on her desk, and he hadn't replied yet to her email telling him she'd made it home safely. His name wasn't up on the chat program, either.

But she had reminders of him everywhere, even if she couldn't see him online. Her desk was covered with glossy photographs, mock-ups of the Franco cologne campaign she'd picked up from Pearce Grey on her way from Euston, and every single one of them had him in it.

She picked up one, a black-and-white shot, and ran her finger over the smooth, cold surface.

Jonny's personality was what made these photographs so captivating—not his body, not his face. It was his pure Jonny-ness.

And none of this was helping her prepare her presentation to Giovanni Franco tomorrow afternoon. Jane exhaled sharply and stood, stretching. Hours on a train and then hours bent over these mock-ups had started an ache in her shoulders and lower back.

Then again, she was used to bending over work. Her back was probably aching because of the unaccustomed exercise of hauling herself up a big old tree.

Like working late on Sunday evening, the ache was worth it. Though it seemed to be joined to an empty ache in her stomach and chest, an ache that hadn't been caused by any exercise.

She walked around her flat, rotating her shoulders and rubbing her neck. She could do with a hot bubble bath and a glass of wine, but that would send her straight to sleep, and she had a good couple of hours' work in front of her still. In the days before Gary had left, she would refocus her mind and refresh her body by lying down on the couch with a bunch of pillows behind her back and watching exactly half an hour of mindless television.

But, of course, Gary had taken both the couch and the television.

'This is ridiculous,' she said, and she strode right back to her desk. Pulling her laptop towards her with one hand, she used the other to type in the website of an online furniture shop.

Half an hour later she was entering her credit card details and specifying a delivery date for her new, overstuffed, soft burgundy velvet sofa and armchair. It didn't match the decoration in the flat, but she figured it was about time she redecorated, anyway. In a way to suit her taste, not anybody else's.

It felt so good that she was just starting to navigate to an electronics site to order a television when her laptop chimed to let her know that someone had just come online.

She was hit by a little hiccup of joy when she saw that it was Jonny.

Working?

The message came up from him right away.

Spending money, actually.

As she typed back she didn't bother to suppress the huge smile that spread across her face.

I wonder if when Licklider came up with the idea of a Galactic Network of computers he ever dreamed that in forty years people would be using the invention to shop and share idle chit-chat with their friends.

Jane laughed aloud.

Jonny, you are such a geek.

Hey, I'm not the one working on a Sunday night.

She picked up the photo of Jonny again and propped it up on her desk.

What are you doing?

I'm wondering something.

What?

It occurred to me that over the past few days, I've told you two of my fantasies. But you haven't told me any of yours.

Jane's fingers had been poised over her keyboard, waiting to give a snappy answer to whatever teasing question he came up with. She froze in position, her eyes locked to the screen.

What are your fantasies, Jane?

Jane swallowed. She looked from her screen to the photograph of Jonny, so like how he was in real life. But not really him, no more than the words on the screen were really him. He was three hundred miles away in Keswick.

My fantasies are all about you.

Tell me.

She leaned her head back on her chair, breathing in deeply from her nose and biting her lip. He had been honest with her, and he was so far away that surely this was safe.

I want to make love with you, Jonny.

I want you to. How?

Slowly. I want to see and touch all of you. I want to fee
and remember every moment. I want to be naked with you

She felt herself blushing furiously. But she also felt a furious
heat in her body that had nothing to do with embarrassment. I
was arousal, and it was freedom.

What else?

Jane closed her eyes and imagined herself with Jonny. The
surroundings didn't matter, as long as it was private, as long a
they could create that little bubble of the two of them. She
imagined standing close to him, taking off his glasses, unfasten
ing each item of his clothing in turn and removing it while he
did the same to her. Their eyes on each other. She imagined him
stroking aside her hair and whispering in her ear, hot words tha
made her body shiver in real life. 'What else?'

I want to tell you what I want.

She barely opened her eyes to look at the screen as she typed
She continued:

I want you to ask me and for me to tell you, every step
of the way.

She shut her eyes again. Imagined speaking the words ou
loud. Letting them live in the air around them. Letting him hear
her, letting him know her. The thought was so tempting that she
shivered again.

A chime from her laptop. She brought herself out of her de
licious dream to the incredible thing that was really happening
in front of her.

Tell me more.

She pulled her laptop closer, as if it were pulling Jonny to her
But it wasn't. The laptop was only plastic and wires, the photo

graphs were only paper. And this was only bytes and bits, an electric conversation in reality as well as in effect.

Do you know what my fantasy really is, though, Jonny? It's being able to tell you this in person. Face to face, to risk it and see your reactions and live it together.

She hit 'send' and she stared at her computer. So many times she had felt as if it was a portal of communication, a line between her and Jonny. Now it felt like a barrier. Another wall she was hiding behind.

There was a knock at her door.

Distracted, aroused, frustrated, she got up and went to her door. She looked through the peephole and there was Jonny, his blue eyes looking steadily at her through his glasses.

CHAPTER FOURTEEN

JANE gasped and took a step back in surprise. Then she opened the door.

Jonny stood in her hallway, tall and beautiful, wearing the same jeans and sweatshirt he'd been wearing during their walk. His laptop was under his arm.

'It was too empty in my flat without you,' he said, and his voice was even richer than she'd been imagining it speaking his words on the screen. 'It was too empty in the whole Lake District without you. So I drove down to London.'

'You've been—'

'Outside your door, hacked into your wireless internet connection. Yes.'

She couldn't quite say anything. Seconds ago she'd been wishing he were right here. And now he was. No need for a computer. All the physical walls down.

'Do you want me to come in?' he asked gently.

She nodded, and then realised that, if she was going to do what she really wanted to do, nodding wasn't a very good start. 'Yes, I want you to come in,' she said.

He stepped in and shut the door behind him, putting his laptop down on the table by the door. They stood looking at each other.

'Tell me what you want to do,' said Jonny.

She reached forward and took off his glasses. The rims were warm from him. She laid them down on the table beside his computer, and then she put her hands on his chest. His heart was beating hard and fast.

'I want you to come into the bathroom with me,' she said. It

ame out without her having planned it, but the minute she said
she knew why she had.

Because she hadn't wanted to take that bubble bath with a
lass of wine. She'd wanted to take it with Jonny.

She took his hand and led him across the living room, through
er bedroom, and into the *en suite* bathroom. 'I want to take a
ath with you,' she said.

'I'd like that, too.'

Turning on the taps, testing the water temperature, pouring
oam bath into the tub—none of that had seemed sexy to Jane
efore. Now, with Jonny watching her every move, close enough
o she could hear him breathing, it seemed just about the sexiest
hing she'd ever done.

She straightened and turned to Jonny. 'I want to undress you,
nd I want you to undress me, too. One piece of clothing at a
me. It was fast, last time, and I want it to be slow.'

'Your wish is my command,' he said, smiling. 'Who gets to
tart?'

'I do.' She unzipped his sweatshirt and pushed it off his shoul-
ers and down his arms, moulding her hands to every muscle she
ncountered as the piece of clothing dropped to the floor. He
vore a plain white T-shirt underneath, fitted enough to empha-
ise his slim build and strong shoulders, loose enough that she
ad to imagine what was underneath.

'My turn?' he asked, and she nodded. He unbuttoned the
ardigan she'd put on to work in, and, like her, pushed it slowly
rom her shoulders and let it fall onto the tiled floor.

'T-shirt,' she said, and she took hold of its hem. He lifted his
rms to help her pull it over his head. She watched, inch by inch,
s she exposed his chest. All that flawless skin, the ribs and
nuscle, the trail of hair on his stomach and the discs of his nipples.

She dropped the shirt on the floor next to their other clothes
nd, though she'd said she'd wanted to take turns removing
lothes, she had to touch him first. Jane put her palms on his
hest, starting at his ribcage. He was warm and solid and real.
lowly, she stroked upwards, feeling his muscles, over his pec-
orals and shoulders. His arms were lean but strong. She cupped

her hands around his biceps, then ran her palms down over hi
corded forearms.

He was so strong. So much stronger than she could ever be.

Jane ran her hands back up Jonny's arms, feeling the way hi
hairs caressed her palms. Back over his shoulders, down hi
chest. She followed the line of hair on his flat stomach downward
and heard him suck in a breath when she got to the top of his low
slung jeans. Here he was paler, the start of the untanned skin she'
noticed the first time they had made love.

'Is it my turn yet?' Jonny asked.

'Not quite.' She grasped his belt buckle and slid the tongu
of his belt out of it. His jeans were button fly and as she unfas
tened them the backs of her fingers brushed against his boxe
shorts and the hot firmness underneath. She pushed his jean
down his legs; he helped her by toeing off his shoes, steppin
out of his jeans, and kicking them aside. Jane squatted down an
pulled his socks off his feet.

She'd never seen his feet. He had gorgeous feet. They wer
well-shaped, with defined tendons and long toes. Even his ankle
were sexy, she decided as she stood, taking her time so she coul
look her fill at his legs on her way up. Not too bulky, but hard an
muscular and masculine, with planes and curves of calf and thigh

'You're distinctly more dressed than I am,' Jonny said.

'It's my fantasy,' she replied, and she tugged his boxer short
down.

Jonny kicked them off, too, and he stood nude in front of her
and Jane couldn't breathe.

Every single inch of him was perfect. Every little bit. Even hi
navel, even his knees. And his penis, so aroused it stood straigh
up in the air, velvet-skinned and intricately veined, was so eve
more than perfect that she bit her lip and had to swallow.

'Jane,' Jonny said gently, and it was only when he spoke tha
she breathed and realised she'd been standing stock-still staring

'You're so incredibly beautiful, Jonny.' Her voice was shaky

'I want to see you, too.'

Involuntarily, she put her hand on her chest. 'I'm not ever
wearing good underwear this time,' she said.

He shrugged and smiled. 'I'm not wearing any.'

'I'm—' She turned abruptly. 'This bath's about to overflow.' She twisted the taps.

She felt a hand on her shoulder. 'Jane,' Jonny said again, and she could hear concern in his voice.

'I'm fine,' she said without thinking, and then she shook her head. It was her fantasy. In her fantasy she told him what she really thought and felt.

Jane turned around again to face Jonny. She tried to look at his face and not at his body, but it didn't make much difference, because his face was just as incredible as the rest of him.

'You're perfect, Jonny,' she said. 'You're a model. And I'm—' She waved her hand over her clothed body, as if her imperfections were too many to count. 'I'm not going to measure up.'

The expression on his face was difficult to understand. It wasn't sympathy, as she'd feared. Instead it was…

It looked suspiciously like incredulity.

'Haven't you figured out yet that you've been my perfect woman all my life?'

The words were unbelievable. But it was impossible to doubt their truth, because they came from Jonny.

'Really?' she couldn't help saying anyway.

'Tell me you want me to take your clothes off, and I'll prove it to you.'

She took a deep breath, and knocked the last of her wall aside.

'I want you to undress me,' she said.

'Finally,' he said, and his tone was so mock-frustrated that she had to laugh.

He began to unbutton her shirt. She watched him deftly handle the buttons, though she kept on being distracted by the fact that his penis nearly brushed her with every movement he made. She couldn't argue with his words, and she couldn't argue with his arousal, either.

She looked into his face. He was concentrating fully on what he was doing as he drew her shirt off her. And she could see it: in the mirror of his eyes, she was perfect.

He caught the silver heart pendant between his fingers. 'You're wearing it underneath your clothes,' he said.

Jane couldn't quite respond to that. The fact that she hadn't taken off the gift he'd given her seemed even more revealing than being naked.

'My bra,' she whispered. He reached round the back and unfastened it, and slid that down her arms, too. She felt her breasts exposed to the warm, steamy air and saw his face become softer, his eyes wider, as if he were looking at something precious.

He touched her, just below her breast, and then on the bottom curve of it. He was warm and gentle and reverent. His thumb ran across her swollen nipple and she pulled in a shuddering breath of pleasure.

'The rest, please,' she said.

She remembered how they had torn at each other's clothes the first time they'd had sex. This couldn't be more different—a slow, meticulous unwrapping. But it was just as sexy, just as overwhelming. Jonny wiggled her jeans down her hips, taking her knickers with them. She wasn't wearing shoes or socks, and she stepped out of her clothes and then settled her feet back on the cool floor.

Jonny straightened. He looked at her. She looked right back at him.

'I've been wanting this for a very long time,' Jonny said.

'Me too.'

Jane felt as if she'd never been truly naked with anyone else, ever before. She held herself still and didn't speak, or cover herself, or turn to see to the bath. She just stood and looked and let Jonny look at her.

They caught each other's eye and both of them smiled.

'Sorry,' Jonny said. 'I can't help staring.'

His appreciation and his desire for her were both so obvious in his face and his body that Jane couldn't help letting out a laugh of amazement and joy. Jonny's smile widened.

She could see it in his eyes. She really was his perfect woman.

'What do you want to do next?' he asked her.

Jane remembered when they'd made love. How he'd touched her and given her pleasure and then surprised and thrilled her by sinking to his knees in front of her.

'I want to see if turnabout is fair play,' she said.

She stepped closer to him and wrapped her hand around his

erection. It leapt in her hand and it felt even harder and hotter than she remembered it. She gave him an experimental stroke, upwards to the head and then back down the shaft to his coarse dark hair, and she heard and felt Jonny catch his breath.

'I want you in my mouth,' she said to him, and at her words his penis throbbed again. The reaction on his face was even sexier, though; his lips parted, his eyes widened, his nostrils flared.

'Okay,' he said, and his voice was low and deep.

His obvious enthusiasm for the idea gave her the courage to say what she was thinking. 'I'm not sure I'm any good at it, though.'

He raised his eyebrows slightly. 'I can't imagine how you could go wrong.'

'I'm just—I've never been very brave.' She flushed, because she knew that sounded stupid. 'I mean, I know that oral sex doesn't require a lot of courage. But I never really felt comfortable enough to experiment.'

Jonny kissed her on her forehead, and then softly on her lips. 'I'd love to be your experimental subject, Jane.' He kissed her again. 'I love your mouth,' he murmured. 'You can't possibly fail.'

Can't possibly fail. She ran her thumb over the tip of his penis and felt the slight moisture that had gathered there, and heard him groan at the back of his throat.

She'd been overtly sexy before with Jonny, but that had been an act. She'd been pretending to be confident in her abilities and desirability, and she'd been following instructions. But this time she was herself. No mistaken identities. This time it was for real.

Jane kissed Jonny on the chest, then downwards. His stomach was rising and falling rapidly with his breathing; the soft hairs tickled her lips. And then she was perched on the side of the tub, her face level with his penis.

He was even more beautiful up close. She relaxed her grip on him and ran just one finger up and down his length, feeling his soft skin, seeing how it stretched over the veins and the hard ridge beneath, how it had a slight curve, how the colour darkened to purple at the tip.

She'd never examined a man like this before, her eyes hungry for every detail. It had always seemed embarrassing. But this was just fascinating. Curious to know what Jonny tasted like, she leaned forward and swiped her tongue lightly over him.

He tasted salty, sweet, but mostly like Jonny. She swirled her tongue around the tip of him, closed her lips over him, and sucked.

'Jane, that's—incredible.'

She was doing it right, then. She licked up the side of his erection as if it were a hard, throbbing lolly and then back down the other side, letting her lips take little nibbles.

Lollies were nice, but never as nice as this. Jane sucked and licked and teased and lapped, darting her tongue against the sensitive head, exploring his contours and ridges. She lightly dragged her teeth against him and he groaned.

'You're very good at this,' he said. His voice was strangled.

Now that she wasn't worried about getting it wrong, she seemed to have a million ideas. Slowly, she took as much of his length inside her mouth as she could, and then, even more slowly, slid him back out again. He felt wonderful inside her mouth. Alive, trusting, restrained strength. His sounds of pleasure encouraged her to go deeper, harder, a little faster.

'I'm not going to be able to stand much more,' he said to her raggedly. She put one of her hands on his thigh to steady herself and she could feel his muscles trembling. Not taking her lips from him, she looked up. His face appeared almost as if he were in pain—his eyebrows drawn together, his eyes unfocused, his bottom lip caught between his teeth.

She was doing that to him, and it felt great. She put her other hand around the base of his penis and stroked him in time with what she was doing with her mouth. Jonny let out a guttural moan and he began to move, tangling his hand in her hair and tensing his thighs, his strength no longer restrained, wild and not gentle, and when he shouted out her name and exploded white-hot into her mouth she felt flooded with power, drenched with pleasure.

And then she felt his hands pulling her up, up to him and he kissed her and wrapped his arms around her and held her to his slick chest. His heart pounded against her breast; his breathing was harsh and quick.

'Was that good?' she asked him, not because she didn't know already, but because she wanted to hear it.

'I think you have a natural talent,' he gasped.

She smiled and rested her head on his chest, feeling his breathing slowly calm, feeling his hands stroking up and down her back from her shoulders to her buttocks and up again.

'Ready for the bath?' she asked him.

'Definitely.'

They stepped into the hot, frothy, scented water and after a few minutes' worth of careful manoeuvring, settled with her legs loosely around his waist and his around hers. She lifted a handful of bubbles and began to spread it over his chest, washing away the perspiration she'd put there.

He scooped up suds himself and caressed them into her shoulders and then, wonderfully, over her breasts. 'You said you're a tomboy but I've never met a tomboy who had bubble bath that smelled like flowers.'

She laughed. The hot water and the smell and Jonny's body and the pleasure she'd just given him aroused her, but relaxed her too. 'My baths have usually been man-free zones.'

'You never took a bath like this with Gary, then?'

'No, never.'

Jonny continued soaping her, but his face was serious. 'Jane, I've got something to tell you.'

'What?' A small stain of apprehension filtered through her contented mood.

'I'm through pretending to be your boyfriend. I'm not going to be anything but honest from now on. But I need to know one thing first.'

'What's that?'

'I need to know that you're not planning to get back together with Gary. That you're really ready to move on.'

She hadn't expected that. She blinked and laughed. 'You're joking. I don't want to get back with Gary.'

A small furrow appeared in his forehead. 'So this whole charade to make him jealous—'

'It wasn't to make Gary jealous. It was to prove that I wasn't a failure.'

'How could you possibly be a failure?'

The question was so simple and said with such genuine puzzlement that she reached forward and gave Jonny a big hug. The water sloshed around them, tickling her breasts as they pressed against his chest.

'I'm no good at relationships, Jonny,' she said when she let him go. 'I never got close enough to Gary to make him love me, and I never let myself really care about him, either. He seemed like the perfect person to marry because we worked so well together, we seemed to get on, and we had interests in common. But it wouldn't have been any sort of a marriage. Much as I hated it, he was right to leave me for somebody who could give him the emotional support he needed.' She sighed. 'I couldn't even relax enough to have a bath with him.'

'And why is it different with me?'

'Because you're you. And I'm not trying to impress you, or live up to anything with you, or have a perfect relationship with you. We're friends.'

'Who are having sex.'

'Well, not right at this minute, but yes.'

'I think that's exactly what we're doing right at this minute.' Jonny's thumbs circled her nipples and sent a shudder of desire through her that raised waves in the soapy water. He raised his legs a little so that she slipped forward, closer to him. She could feel his penis, erect again, resting on her stomach below her belly button.

Then he slid his hand downward into the water. Between her legs.

Jane gasped. She hadn't quite known how much she craved him there, until he was touching her. The water lapped against her along with his fingers; it was all hot, liquid pleasure as he parted her.

'Jonny,' she whimpered. She leant back on his thighs, bent up at the knee, and spread her legs wider for him. Quickly, more quickly than she'd thought possible, he was sending tremors through her body. He slid a finger of his other hand inside her, touching her inside and out with long, sensuous movements, and Jane, transported just like that from cosy intimacy to desperate sexual need, moaned and lifted her hips even closer to him.

'We're more than just friends, Jane,' Jonny said. The words floated in the steamy air of the bathroom and Jane tried to focus on them, but the exquisite sensations he was producing made it difficult for her to think of anything but his hands, his body, him.

Not stopping his movements, he leaned forward and fastened his mouth onto one of her nipples, already super-sensitive from his ministrations with the bath foam.

That was it. Her climax burst from her, her hips bucking right out of the water. The waves, the hot foamy water around her, Jonny's arms and legs and his mouth and his fingers, it all became far, far too good. She yelled and thrashed and spilt water all over and heard him chuckle in male satisfaction.

He pulled her to him, wrapped his arms and legs tightly around her as she quivered with the aftershocks of pleasure. With a wet hand, he smoothed her damp hair back from her face.

'Much more than friends,' he murmured in her ear.

She felt boneless against him. Jonny repositioned them and lifted her out of the tub to set her on her feet. He took a thick towel from the rail and wrapped her in it. The material was soft and rough at once on her over-sensitised skin; when he rubbed it against her breasts and between her legs she shuddered again.

'I want you,' she told him, and pulled a towel off the rail to dry him, too. His glorious, golden body, all muscle and sinew and sculpted bone. His beautiful, masculine face, intent on every curve and swell of her own body.

'Inside me,' she added, though it wasn't really necessary; from his expression and from his blatant arousal, she was sure he knew exactly what she meant.

'Yes. Bed. Now.' He grabbed her hand and they ran from the bathroom and fell on the bed and they were kissing each other, lips and tongues frantic, limbs tangled, their damp skin clinging.

'I want to be on top,' she panted, and Jonny rolled onto his back. Quickly, breathless, Jane straddled him and reached over to her bedside table for a condom.

'Do you want it slow or fast?' he asked her, and the question was so damn sexy that she yanked the drawer open with a jerk that shook the table, tipping the phone and a half-empty glass of water onto the floor. The glass hit the carpet with a thunk, the phone fell off its receiver and buzzed a dial tone.

She didn't care. Jane fished inside the drawer until she came up with a condom, which she held up in triumph to show to Jonny. He laughed as she ripped the packet open with her teeth, and then gasped when she stroked the latex down on him.

Jane positioned herself above him, feeling the head of his erection at her entrance. She wanted to push down hard, impale herself on him, feel him all the way through her body, and she was about to do it when she paused.

Slow or fast? They'd already done it fast. Slow would be more of an adventure.

So she lowered herself just a little bit, just enough to take the tip of him inside her. The tip of him where she knew he was most sensitive, where she'd let her tongue and lips linger. She squeezed her muscles around him and he gasped.

And then, a hair's breadth at a time, down onto him. So, so slowly feeling herself part around him, accept him, surround him. Until she was all the way down, resting against his body, the full length of him buried inside her. She circled her hips, savouring his hardness and the way his body rubbed against her, creating sweet friction on her thighs and on her clitoris. And then she stayed still.

'Slow,' she said.

He was smiling at her. 'You're incredible,' he said.

'I never thought I was very good at sex.' Deliberate circles, squeezing him deep within her.

'You are.'

She decided it was time to slide up on him again, feel the long, hard extent of him, and then take him all back in. Slowly. Good, and even better because Jonny was looking her straight in the eyes, half a smile of happiness on his face.

Being in control was incredible. Like flying, like whooping out in joy, like coming up with the best idea in the history of advertising, except right now she could share this. It wasn't just her victory. It was something they were building together.

Because she was in control, but Jonny was definitely in this with her. He put his fingers on her again. Jane leaned back, tilting her crotch up towards his clever hand, her hands balanced on his thighs. But she couldn't stay still; her hips, following a rhythm of their own, moved restlessly back and forth, and she felt her muscles contracting with every movement of his hand.

And ripples began to course through her body, again much, much sooner than she would have expected.

This time, as her orgasm possessed her, she fell forward, her hands planted on Jonny's chest, and thrust herself down on him hard. He filled her, he kissed her, and she cried out into his mouth.

She couldn't tell how long it lasted after that. It was a timeless, endless expanse of pleasure. Her control was gone, shattered by wave after wave of ecstasy sweeping through her. She felt his hands on her hips, lifting her and grinding her body against him; she felt him moving inside her, bringing her to even greater heights. She heard her voice, panting out incoherent pleas for more, and Jonny was everything and everywhere.

At some point he rolled over on top of her, his whole body bearing down on her, his hands holding hers above her head as he thrust still slowly into her, making it last, and yet another orgasm seized her, or maybe the last one hadn't ended, and she wrapped her legs around his waist and hung on for dear life.

And then he was holding her face in his hands and holding her eyes with his own, so intense yet so gentle, and he said, simply, 'Jane,' and even though she felt him pulse inside her, felt his body shudder against her, mostly she saw his orgasm in his eyes.

His eyelids opening slightly, his pupils dilating, the blue of his irises becoming even more electric. As if he was looking even deeper into her, and giving her something even more of himself.

Then he collapsed onto her, and she hugged him, feeling their heartbeats pounding together.

'Wow,' Jonny said into the pillow.

She nodded, unable to speak.

He rolled over and pulled her to his side, tucking her under his arm. She curled up against him. How had she ever been scared about being naked with Jonny? It was the best, most natural feeling in the world.

She kissed the side of his face and closed her eyes.

'Am I still a geek?' he whispered.

'You're you,' she answered, and rode along on a cloud of bliss into sleep.

CHAPTER FIFTEEN

HER pillow was warm and firm, and was rising and falling with a soft whooshing sound.

Jane opened her eyes to a close-up view of Jonny's chest. From here, with her cheek pressed to the hollow of his shoulder, it was a landscape of swells and dips, muscles and nipples, and just about the best thing she'd ever opened her eyes to in the morning.

She twisted her head and looked at his face. He was propped up on a pillow, gazing down at her.

'How long have you been awake?' she asked.

'A while.' He twisted his fingers in her hair and brushed it back. 'I like watching you sleep.'

She quickly touched her mouth, afraid she'd drooled on him or something.

'You didn't leave a wet patch and I wouldn't care if you did,' he told her. 'You didn't snore or kick me, either, before you ask.'

The thought had crossed her mind. Jane stretched and yawned. Jonny's chest was surprisingly comfortable, considering it was a lot harder than the pillow she was used to. He tilted her chin up and kissed her.

She was just about to relax into the kiss when she remembered she hadn't even brushed her teeth before falling asleep last night. 'Morning breath,' she said, putting her fingers over her lips.

He took her hand away from her mouth. 'You don't have to be perfect, Jane. Being here with you is everything I want. Morning breath and all.'

This time when he kissed her, she did relax. The man really

did know how to kiss: gentle, and yet with enough passion so that she could remember their frantic, carnal kisses of the night before.

Desire rose in her, lazy but insistent, and she made a needy sound in the back of her throat as he rolled them both over and covered her with his warm, heavy body. She wrapped her arms and legs around him and loved how wonderful his skin felt against hers. And how his morning erection was pressed into her thigh.

Her eyes flew open, for the first time appreciating the daylight streaming into the room. Morning. It was morning, and she hadn't set an alarm last night.

'What time is it?' she gasped.

Jonny looked over at the clock. 'Just past ten.'

Instinct made her tense, and Jonny shifted his weight so he wasn't pressing her down. 'Is that a problem?' he asked.

She struggled to sit up—not easy, because her muscles were tired from what she'd got up to last night, and her body wasn't eager to be hauled away from Jonny. 'I usually get into work for eight. But I can have flexitime if I want.'

'But you've never taken it before.'

'It's fine.' She ran her fingers through her hair, trying to put it into some semblance of order. 'I've got the big meeting with Giovanni Franco and his team, but that's not until after lunch. Besides, if anybody needs to get in touch with me, they can always ring—oh.'

She spotted the empty space where her phone had been, and remembered it had been on the floor, off the hook, since she'd knocked it off in her search for birth control.

'They can ring my mobile,' she corrected herself.

'So you can spend more time here in bed with me,' Jonny said, and wrapped his arm around her bare waist.

She melted. She couldn't help it. It was as if her body had an automatic 'plaster yourself all over Jonny' button and he'd just pushed it. She lay back in his arms and let him curl her up into his warmth.

She expected him to kiss her again, but instead he caressed her face. His hands were big and masculine, yet sensitive, and a mere touch of her cheek made her close her eyes in pleasure for a moment. When she opened them again, he was gazing intently into her eyes.

'You remember last night when I said I was through pretending to be your boyfriend?' he said.

She thought back. She'd been a little distracted by all his glorious nakedness and all the orgasms and such, but she did remember him saying something like that.

'It doesn't matter,' she said. 'It was a stupid thing to do anyway. And it bothered you. I'm sorry.'

'The reason I'm not going to pretend any more is because I intend to be your boyfriend for real. I'm not going to fool around and say that I'm your friend who you happen to be having sex with. Because I don't feel like that, Jane. I love you.'

Her heart and stomach and mind leapt, and her body actually startled in his arms, with a feeling that was nearly joy, nearly fulfilment, nearly like flying.

And then, just as quickly, she fell back to earth. Her heart thumped painfully, her stomach sank so that she felt as if she might be sick.

'We can take it slowly,' he was saying to her. 'I know you've just finished with an engagement and I'm living up north for the next little while at least, until I make sure the hotel isn't in trouble any more. But I love you, Jane, and I've loved you for years, and I'm tired of trying to hide it.'

Oh…he'd never hidden it.

She stared, frozen, into his eyes and she knew that he had been looking at her this way from the very first moment she'd seen him again. The warmth wasn't just friendship, not merely the way Jonny was. It was because he loved her.

It was like the photographs of his parents on his mother's wall. Something open, honest, and true. Something with expectations of for ever.

And Jonny was watching her, wanting her to say something back to him.

'I—' *I don't know how to give you for ever.*

She bit her lip, and swallowed.

'I'm sorry, Jonny, can we talk about this later?' she said. 'I just remembered I never finished the slides for my presentation this afternoon.'

'Slides,' he said.

'Yes. I was working on them when you—when we talked online.' She slipped out of his arms and sat up. Her robe was in the wardrobe, across the room. Her underwear drawer was closer. As quickly as she could, she bolted out of bed and to her chest of drawers, and got a pair of knickers and a bra on. She felt Jonny's eyes on her the entire time.

'Are you all right?' he asked her.

'Fine,' she said, crossing to her wardrobe, then winced as she realised the word she'd used. 'I mean, I'm a little stressed out about work. I don't usually—'

'Go in late. I know. But I thought you agreed you deserved some time off every now and then.'

'I do.' She pulled out a suit and a blouse, without checking to see if they matched, and began to put them on. She hadn't showered, but, right at this moment, getting covered up seemed more important than getting clean.

'And I had a wonderful time last night, Jonny. It's just that I'm not only late, but I'm unprepared. So I need to go in and get it sorted out.'

She glanced at him, sitting up in her bed. His feelings about her were naked on his face. So were sadness and disappointment.

Her stomach twisted and she felt even more sick.

'I'm sorry, Jonny, I know you want to talk, but let's talk later, okay?' She escaped into the bathroom before she could hear what he had to say.

But the bathroom wasn't any escape. The floor was littered with her clothes, and his; the bath was still full of water, now cold and flat; the whole room was full of drunken memories of their touching, their kissing, their laughing.

Their making love. For Jonny, in the truest sense.

She hurried to wash her face, brush her teeth, pin up her hair, and to swipe on some make-up, and then she went from the frying-pan into the fire because, although the bathroom was full of reminders of Jonny, the bedroom was full of him.

She was talking even before she entirely entered the room. 'Were you planning to go back to Cumbria today, or will you stay a little longer? I'll probably have to work through lunch, but we can do dinner, if you like.'

'Jane.' He was out of bed, and he intercepted her halfway across the room. Of course he was still nude, still warm from bed, still smelling of Jonny and bubble bath and the sex they'd shared, and she smelled like that too. She was going to smell like that at work.

She bit her lip, caught between present pain and future embarrassment.

Jonny put one hand on her shoulder, one hand on her face. 'I meant what I said. I don't mind taking it slowly. If it were up to me, I'd blazon it from the rooftops. But I can wait for you, if I need to.' He smiled wryly, something that was just as sexy as his naked body. 'I've been waiting for you since I was about nine years old, a little while longer won't hurt. Much.'

Maybe it wouldn't hurt much. Until he discovered what she was really like, who she really was. She nodded and stepped back from him.

'Let's have dinner. I need to go now, Jonny.' She kissed him swiftly on the cheek. 'Help yourself to whatever you can find in the flat. There's an extra key in the cabinet with the glasses if you need to go out and come back. I'll ring you later, all right?'

And she fled.

Jonny prowled around the flat. Without a couch, there wasn't any place comfortable to rest, except for the bath, the bed, and the desk chair. And all of them held too many memories right now, of Jane confiding in him, Jane touching him, Jane telling him what she wanted and blowing his mind.

And none of those memories quite blocked out the reality of Jane hearing that he loved her and immediately running a mile.

She'd suggested dinner. He snorted, walking from the window to the kitchen to pour himself a glass of water and back again to the window. What good was dinner going to do? As if it were their first date again. No, not even that: as if it were a business meeting. They could have dinner and he just bet that Jane would spend

he entire evening talking about subjects unrelated to the two of
hem, avoiding facing their relationship as she had this morning.

Or else, she'd be as she had been on their actual first date, and
grab him to have wild sex with her before they actually got to
dinner. He knew which one he'd prefer, but even the second
option didn't give him what he really needed.

Which was her. Not her presence, not her body, but her.

He slammed his water on the nearest table, hard enough to
splash some of it out of the glass.

What did she want? She didn't want Gary, he understood that
now. She didn't want the fake relationship they'd been putting
on. But she didn't want a real relationship, either.

'So what the hell am I supposed to do?' he asked the view of
London.

He heard the familiar ringing of his mobile phone, and his
heart nearly leapt out of his chest. He grabbed it off the desk
where he'd left it and he was so sure it was Jane he didn't even
bother to check the number on the screen before he pressed the
button and said, 'Jane?'

'Dude, you are totally lovesick.'

'Thom.' He didn't succeed in hiding his disappointment.
'How are you?'

'Well, that depends what standpoint you're judging from. I
had an awesome weekend.'

'That's good,' he said automatically, leaning against the
window frame and looking out at London again. The day was
overcast, about as grey as he felt.

'No, more than good. Awesome. I've had nearly enough sex
to last me till the next leap year. And then on Sunday, Amy's kid
Stacy came back from her dad's and we went to the London
Aquarium. I tell you, I've never seen a kid who liked jellyfish
that much.'

Jonny dragged himself away from his own frustration enough
to think about what Thom was saying. 'Does this mean you're
not so bothered about Amy being a mother?'

'Well, in theory, yeah. I mean, it's not like I ever set out to be
somebody's dad or anything. But in practice, she's an excellent

kid. I haven't laughed so much in ages. And watching Amy with her—you know, it's sort of incredible.'

'Is this your way of telling me that you and Amy might be something more than sex friends?'

'Dude. I will plead the Fifth Amendment on account of the fact that the information may be personally incriminating. But I will say that I'm glad I decided to grow the London business for the next year or two.'

'Good.' Jonny smiled.

'Yeah, that's the good standpoint. From the other standpoint, it's all going tits-up. What does Jane say?'

He stood up straight. 'What does Jane say about what?'

'Oh. I thought you'd have talked to her. According to Amy, strange things are afoot at Pearce Grey and your girlfriend is in the middle of it.'

The minute Jane stepped inside the door she knew something wasn't right.

At first she thought it was because of her, as if her time with Jonny had transformed her perspective of the world so hugely that even her office seemed to be a whole different world. The familiar tube journey had seemed strange, too; she was unable to focus on the easy, everyday actions such as swiping her pass on the sensor at the barrier or threading her way through commuters coming off the train she wanted to board. The train had stopped once between stations and whereas normally she wouldn't even register the short delay, using the time to think through a work issue in her head, this time she shifted in her seat and tapped her feet and hands, feeling as though the stalled movement was stopping her from getting on, from moving away from Jonny and what he had said to her and all the doubts and fears that his declaration had caused.

And the joy. Sitting in the stopped train, forced by stillness to examine her own feelings, she had to admit that for an unguarded moment, hearing that Jonathan Cole loved her had made her the happiest she had ever felt.

That revelation had made the journey seem even more surreal, even after the train got going again.

And now Pearce Grey was quiet. Much quieter than usual on a Monday morning. The few people who were sitting at desks in the big open-plan workspace swivelled their heads toward her as soon as she walked in, and she could have sworn she heard a sharp intake of breath from someone. Hasan, who had his ear to a telephone but wasn't speaking, jumped out of his chair.

Before Hasan could get to her, the door to the boardroom opened and Gary practically ran out. She'd never seen him look so frantic and upset. Not even when he'd been breaking up with her.

'Jane!' he cried. 'Where have you been?'

'At home,' she answered. 'What's the matter?'

'Giovanni Franco rescheduled the meeting for this morning. Didn't you get any of our messages?'

'What messages?' She glanced at the glass wall of the boardroom. Most of the team were there, and not only the team from the design firm, but Giovanni Franco himself. She recognised him from the back of his silver-haired head.

'We've been trying to get in touch with you since last night. Your phones are off.'

She remembered her landline, buzzing a dial tone next to her bed while she and Jonny had got on with more interesting things.

'My mobile should be working,' she said, and put her hand in her bag to pull it out.

It was off.

And then she remembered—she'd turned it off on Sunday, before she and Jonny had gone on their walking and tree-climbing and kissing expedition. And she'd been too distracted by Jonny to think about turning it back on again.

'I sent you about twenty emails,' Hasan said from beside her.

She hadn't looked at those, either, because even though her computer had been switched on, she'd been too busy talking sexual fantasies to notice any incoming mail.

She'd felt sick all morning, but now her stomach felt as if it were scrambling to escape from her body any way it could, pre-ferably through her feet.

'When did the meeting start?' she asked, her voice barely audible.

'At nine,' said Gary. 'Franco's PA rang me yesterday to re-schedule it. I had to book an earlier flight from Milan to get back here in time to warn everyone.'

Everyone except for her.

She swallowed, and then adopted a brisk tone. 'Well, I'm here now.' She began walking towards the boardroom. 'How has it gone so far?'

'Terrible.' Gary was speaking quietly, so the people in the boardroom couldn't hear. 'You've got all the mock-ups. Amy's been in since six or so and she's cobbled together what she could, and it's good, but not as good as it should have been.'

Guilt stabbed through her. It wasn't just her mistake; this made everyone on the team look bad. And they didn't deserve it.

'Anyway, I'm sure it will be all right if you go in and give him your presentation. Giovanni Franco is just about spitting nails, but you're bound to impress him.'

Jane stopped. 'But I didn't finish my presentation.'

Gary's eyes just about bugged out of his head. It wasn't an attractive look. 'You always finish your presentations days before they're due.'

'I didn't this time. I thought—'

They had reached the boardroom by this time. It was very quiet in there. Quiet enough so that the team, and Franco's team, and Franco himself, might have heard her conversation with Gary.

Through the door and the glass wall, she could see Amy, looking flustered and upset, with her laptop and a projector and her sketches for the campaign. Jane hated to think about what kind of morning she had had, trying desperately to find child-care for Stacy and put together a presentation because Jane herself had dropped the ball.

A chair scraped slowly back in the silence, and Giovanni Franco rose and turned to face Jane. She had met him before, but she'd never seen him looking like this, like a thundercloud personified.

'Ms Miller,' he said. His voice was shattered-glass anger. 'How nice of you to join us. I didn't think it unreasonable that you would turn up for your own client meeting, prepared for your client.'

'I'm very sorry, Mr Franco. I didn't get the message that you had changed it, and I believed it was this afternoon. If you'd like to look at what I do have for you—'

He held up a hand. 'Don't bother. I thought, when I commissioned Pearce Grey, that you were a professional organisation. But the treatment I've received this morning has proven otherwise. I've wasted two hours here and seen nothing of value.'

'Mr Franco, we are a professional organisation. And the campaign we have designed for you is absolutely stunning. Our team has produced work that I'm very proud of. Let me show you what I have, and we can set up another meeting to go through this in more detail.'

'*This* was the meeting I had arranged, Ms Miller. And your team has not impressed me.' He waved his hand at her dismissively and made to walk past her through the door.

Her guts stopped trying to escape from her body. Instead, they hit her with a rush of adrenaline, a hot punch of anger.

'Mr Franco,' she said, her voice loud and clear and strong, 'I'm sorry you are disappointed and I apologise for my role in that. But my team are outstanding and if you are not happy, it's purely because you moved the goalposts at the last minute. They have been working day and night to get your campaign ready for you today, even though we normally don't hold meetings such as this without the partners present, because you requested it. The account manager, Mr Kaplan, rearranged his holiday weekend in order to accommodate your wishes. And my art director has gone beyond the call of duty to get her materials ready to present to you several hours before you asked for them.'

'Which is no less than I'd expect,' he said.

'Of course. Your business is important to us. But you changed the meeting time on Sunday afternoon, Mr Franco. A time most people want to spend with their family or loved ones. My team worked extremely hard for you, and they deserve a little bit of time for themselves without having their mobile phones constantly turned on in case you want to tell them to jump higher.'

She stopped, out of words. The silence was absolute.

'I see,' said Mr Franco, slowly. 'Thank you for instructing me on business practices. I can see that our organisations' policies are not compatible, Ms Miller. It's a pity that after all your extremely hard work, I shan't be requiring your campaign after all.'

This time he did sweep by her. Jane watched, dumbly, as his team followed him out through the door. Not one of them looked her in the eye.

All at once, her adrenaline and her anger deserted her. She gripped the side of the door to support her boneless body.

She'd just single-handedly lost her company this and every future Giovanni Franco campaign.

Jane turned around before she could see what the people in the boardroom, and the entire company, thought of her. Blindly, she groped past the desks and chairs across the open-plan office to the fire-escape door, opposite to the direction the designer and his minions had just taken. Then she was in the bare staircase, down a short flight of stairs into an alley at the back of the building.

For a moment, she leaned back against the wall, just breathing. Franco would be in the front of the building, getting a cab or having his car pick him up. She didn't suppose he did anything so ordinary as walking or getting a bus. She counted minutes in her head, trying to force out other thoughts. It was quiet in this alley, and more private than her office, but sooner or later someone would find her here, and getting the reputation of skulking in alleyways after blowing her firm's most important contract of the year would not help her to get another job.

Then again, as she might not ever work in advertising again, maybe her reputation didn't matter.

She groaned and pushed herself off the wall. Giovanni Franco must be gone by now, and she needed to go somewhere, anywhere, to think. She went round the corner to the main road and by instinct struck out in the direction she'd come from this morning, towards the tube station, as if by retracing her steps she could rewind what had happened, what she had done.

She should never have agreed to go away for the weekend. Never switched off her phone. Never given in to the temptation of Jonny, thought about her own selfish pleasure instead of her team who were depending on her, never messed around with something and somebody that was only going to lead to disaster—

Jane walked full-tilt into something. Someone. Someone who wrapped arms around her. She tried to push away, looked up, realised it was Jonny, hair rumpled, glasses askew from the force of their collision.

Her insides soared, then plunged. Jonny, who loved her. Whom she'd hurt this morning. Who was looking at her with concern that she knew she didn't deserve.

'What's happened?' he asked. He didn't even bother to straighten his glasses, just held onto her, firmly but carefully, as if she were precious.

As if.

'I blew the Giovanni Franco campaign. They rescheduled the meeting and I didn't know because I had my phones turned off and I wasn't checking my emails. And I hadn't finished the presentation. And I told Franco that he couldn't demand our staff to be on call for him twenty-four hours a day. So he cancelled the whole thing.'

Saying the words aloud made them even more real, made her flesh creep with dread.

'Well, you were right,' Jonny said.

He said it so simply, so matter-of-factly, as if she could flush her career down the toilet without a single backwards glance. As if it didn't matter.

'No, I wasn't!' she cried. 'It wasn't right at all, none of it. I'm not a helpless incompetent female who gets all emotional and screws up. I'm—'

She stuttered to a halt. Because that was precisely what she was, wasn't it? An emotional female who'd screwed up and was now in the middle of a busy pavement, having her hands held and being comforted by a big, strong man?

She snatched her hands away from Jonny.

'I can't live this way,' she said.

'Jane, don't be silly.'

Anger made her teeth clench. 'I'm not silly.'

'No, you're right. You're not silly. You're the most incredible woman I know.' He touched her again, drew her stiff body into the warmth of his arms. 'I love you and we'll work it out.'

As if love were the answer. As if love would protect you from failure or humiliation. As if love could just be there, to be relied on, without you having to earn it.

She struggled free of him. He was so damn certain of himself, so stubborn, so male.

'Prove it.'

'Look at my parents, look at what they had to deal with, and they were happy.'

'I'm not like that, Jonny!' she cried. 'That's the whole problem. You want too much of me and I can't give it to you. I can't do the wedding and the happy family. I just don't know how. I've never had it and I don't know the rules. I can't drop who I am and become this person who wastes time climbing trees and thinking about sex and trying to love someone.'

She'd thrown the words out, fast and hard, as if she were constructing a wall with them, and from the way Jonny flinched she knew that some of them had hit home. For a moment, satisfaction flared in her, that she had pierced, somehow, his strength.

'You think that trying to love me is a waste of time?' he said. And Jonny didn't hide how he felt. Every word was raw with hurt, and with anger.

The satisfaction drained away more quickly than it had come. Instead, she filled with pain, twisting her heart, pricking at her eyes.

She backed away. Blinking, blinking. Because if the tears fell it was admitting total defeat.

'I have to go back to work,' she said.

'So you can pretend that everything's all right again?' He lashed out as she had done, and the challenge made her snap back.

'Everything was all right until you came along! If I hadn't met you none of this would have happened!'

'And you would've been stuck in your little "fine" world?'

'Yes!'

She'd stepped several feet back, her fists clenched, her heart hammering, and she shouted the last word. Passers-by stared at her, looked quickly away, deviated from their course to give her a wide berth.

'I don't want to do this here,' she said. 'I'm finished.'

She turned on her heel and started walking. After only one or two steps, Jonny caught her and turned her around to face him.

'Jane, the answer to this is simple, and you've been playing around and avoiding the question and using work as an excuse from the moment I've met you. Do you love me?'

His face was so open. She could see the pain, and the frustration. And the love, too. The love that had never left, and that made it hard for her to breathe, made her think of failure.

'I don't even know what that means,' she whispered.

His eyes narrowed, his lips thinned. His expression closed.

'And you don't want to find out.' He let her go, dropped his hands. 'Go ahead and go back to work.'

'Jonny,' she said, 'without my job I'm nothing.'

'Jane,' he said, and he was, at that moment, the angriest she had ever seen him, 'if you really believe that, maybe it's true. Goodbye.'

He turned and walked away.

She should have felt free. Instead she felt like what Jonny had just called her.

Nothing.

Jane turned around again and forced herself back towards Pearce Grey. She might be a failure, but she wasn't a coward. She would apologise to everyone concerned—the whole company, if necessary. And then she'd start racking her brains to come up with damage-limitation strategies.

Walking and having something definite to do, even something so awful, made her tears less imminent. Jane opened the door, nodded at Melinda the receptionist, who was staring at her openly, and went up the short flight of stairs to the office proper. Before she stepped into sight she took a deep breath, smoothed her suit, made sure her hair was tidy. When she raised her hands near her face she smelled the indefinable, clean scent that was Jonny.

She shook her head and took the final step into the office, with all of the team she had let down.

The room wasn't silent this time; it was abuzz, full of people. But again, heads swivelled when she entered, and she heard someone say, 'Jane!'

And then she heard something incredible.

Applause.

The entire staff of Pearce Grey stood up behind their desks and raised their hands and clapped, smiling at her.

Jane froze, staring. Amy detached herself from a group near the centre of the room and ran to Jane, her arms outstretched.

'Woman!' she cried, throwing her arms around Jane and giving her a huge, perfumed squeeze. 'You rule!'

'What?'

Amy leaned back, still hugging Jane. 'The way you stuck up for us with Franco! You said exactly what every single one of us wanted to say but were afraid to.'

'But—I lost the contract.'

'Stuff his contract! Who wants to work for a client who can't be bothered to trust your judgement? Giovanni has worked with six agencies in the past three years and never once had an advertising campaign that he stood behind one hundred per cent. He thinks he wants edgy, but then he gradually chips away at the campaign until it's nothing but a compromise. My friend works for Hinterland who did his last womenswear campaign. She said it was a nightmare and they were relieved when he decided to look elsewhere.'

'But it's a huge source of revenue for the company—high profile—and our reputation—'

'Given his history, being fired by Giovanni Franco might do our reputation more good in the long run.' Gary had appeared by her side. 'I've got a conference call scheduled with both of our partners this afternoon and I'm planning on backing your conduct one hundred per cent. They might not be happy, but they'll have to take all of their employees' feelings into account.'

'And we all feel the same way,' Amy told her. 'Sometimes there are things that are more important than work. Like principles, and a life, and your friends.'

Jane stared around the room. All of these people, whom she'd tried so hard to put a perfect face on with, to be all professional, all of the time—all of them were smiling at her. Applauding her.

Agreeing that they were her friends.

And yet she still felt empty. Like a big zero. Nothing. Because in a room full of friends, she couldn't think about anybody except for Jonny, her best friend and her lover. Walking away.

'Oh, my God,' she said. 'What have I done?'

In the end, it was Amy who tracked him down, after Jane tried phone calls and emails and got nowhere. Jane called Thom's mobile.

'Uh, no, no idea where he might be,' Thom said, and the tone of his voice made him sound as if he were shifting around uncomfortably in his seat, wherever that was. 'None at all. Nope. Sorry. Good luck.'

'He's a lousy liar,' Amy told her when Jane hung up and reported the conversation. 'He tried pretending he didn't care about the fact that I had a daughter, too. Utterly unconvincing. Come on, I know where he is.'

'Where is he?' Jane asked, following Amy out of her office, the two of them stopping to pick up Amy's voluminous handbag.

'At my flat looking after Stacy. She had a dicky tummy this morning and I couldn't stay home with her because of evil Franco man.'

'Thom's babysitting?'

'He said he didn't know how, but I could see he was dying to. They get on like a house on fire. Speaking of which, I hope they haven't tried using the gas cooker.'

Amy's face, as she said this, was radiant.

A cab ride later Jane was standing next to Amy as she unlocked the door to her flat. She bit her lip and twisted her hands together. She didn't feel empty any more.

She felt terrified.

'If the Franco cologne campaign had gone forward and been extended, Jonny would be looking at earning some serious money,' she told Amy. 'But when I told him it had fallen through he didn't even think about himself. He only cared about how I felt about it.'

'He's a keeper,' Amy said, and swung the door open. 'What the—?'

The door opened straight into the living room of the flat. Jane had never been here before and she knew that creative people were often chaotic, but she doubted that Amy was usually as chaotic as this. The floor was strewn with clothes, a laundry basket was overturned on the floor, and the ironing-board, with its legs not extended, lay on the carpet. Thom was carefully balanced on it, his arms outstretched and his knees bent, while Stacy sat on the pointed front.

'What are you two doing?' Amy asked.

Thom leaped off the ironing-board. 'Uh, I was teaching Stacy how to surf.'

Amy put her hands on her hips. 'If you're well enough to surf, young lady, you're well enough to go to school.'

'Yeah, that's what I told her,' said Thom quickly. He caught Jane's eye and jerked his head in the direction of the next room. *Kitchen,* he mouthed.

Jane threaded her way through the laundry and went into the kitchen. Jonny was sitting at the table, with a mug of tea in front of him.

She had to catch her breath. Because he was perfect. Hair rumpled, chin rough, wearing clothes that had spent the night on a damp bathroom floor. Every single inch of him was exactly everything she had ever wanted a man to be.

He looked up when she entered and their eyes met. It was like electricity. And it didn't make her any less terrified.

'I'm sorry,' she said.

Jonny stood. 'Jane, I shouldn't have said—'

'No, wait.' She held up her hand and Jonny stopped. He didn't need to say anything anyway because she could tell exactly what he was thinking from the look on his face.

'I'm frightened of loving you,' she said. 'I messed things up with Gary and I never loved him. If I lost you, I couldn't bear it.'

He pushed his chair aside and came a step closer to her. 'You're not going to lose me.'

She held up her hand again. 'I don't understand why you love me. I don't think I've earned it. I keep on messing things up with you. I'm completely clueless about relationships. I didn't even know I had friends until I did something that made me sure I was going to lose all of them.'

Her eyes prickled. The tears she'd held back for so long because she didn't want anybody to see. One of them fell. She didn't care. She could cry with Jonny. She didn't have anything to lose. And, maybe, everything to gain.

'So I have a theory,' she said, wiping her eyes, 'and maybe you can tell me if it's right. I wondered if maybe I didn't have to earn your love. Because you didn't have to do anything to make me love you. You just had to be yourself.'

This time she couldn't have stopped him if she'd wanted to. He was across the kitchen and he had pulled her into his arms and he was kissing her in that exciting, passionate, tender way that only Jonny could kiss. Smearing her tears on her face, warming her entire body and heart and soul.

When it was over he smiled at her. No, he beamed at her.

'You only have to be yourself, Jane,' he said to her, and wiped her eyes for her.

This time, she believed it. She beamed back, through her drying tears, full of love and joy and the possibility of a happy ending.

And mischief, too. 'What's your wildest fantasy, Jonny?' she asked him.

'Marrying you. Being together. Talking with you. Having adventures. Raising kids. Being happy.'

'Okay. We can do that. But what I meant was—' and she leaned forward, touched his upper lip with her tongue, and asked the rest of the question in a husky murmur that made Jonny's hands tighten on her, and made his eyes take on that sexy gleam '—what's your wildest fantasy that I can start making come true tonight?'

Jonny began to whisper in her ear.

Don't miss favorite author

Michelle Reid's

next book, coming in May 2008,
brought to you only
by Harlequin Presents!

THE MARKONOS BRIDE

#2723

Aristos is bittersweet for Louisa: here, she met
and married gorgeous Greek playboy Andreas
Markonos and produced a precious son. After
tragedy, Louisa was compelled to leave.
Five years later, she is back....

*Look out for more spectacular stories
from Michelle Reid, coming soon in 2008!*

HARLEQUIN *Presents*

Be sure not to miss favorite
Harlequin Romance author

Lucy Gordon

in Harlequin Presents—
for one month only in May 2008!

THE ITALIAN'S
PASSIONATE
REVENGE

#2726

Elise Carlton is wary of being a trophy wife—except
to rich, well-dressed and devastatingly handsome
Vincente Farnese. It is no coincidence that this dark
Italian has sought her out for seduction....

Coming in June 2008 in Harlequin Romance:

The Italian's Cinderella Bride
by Lucy Gordon

www.eHarlequin.com

HP12726

REQUEST YOUR FREE BOOKS!

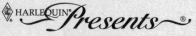

2 FREE NOVELS
PLUS 2
FREE GIFTS!

YES! Please send me 2 FREE Harlequin Presents® novels and my 2 FREE gifts (gifts are worth about $10). After receiving them, if I don't wish to receive any more books, I can return the shipping statement marked "cancel." If I don't cancel, I will receive 6 brand-new novels every month and be billed just $4.05 per book in the U.S. or $4.74 per book in Canada, plus 25¢ shipping and handling per book and applicable taxes, if any*. That's a savings of close to 15% off the cover price! I understand that accepting the 2 free books and gifts places me under no obligation to buy anything. I can always return a shipment and cancel at any time. Even if I never buy another book, the two free books and gifts are mine to keep forever.

106 HDN ERRW 306 HDN ERRL

Name _____ (PLEASE PRINT)

Address _____ Apt. #

City _____ State/Prov. _____ Zip/Postal Code

Signature (if under 18, a parent or guardian must sign)

Mail to the **Harlequin Reader Service:**
IN U.S.A.: P.O. Box 1867, Buffalo, NY 14240-1867
IN CANADA: P.O. Box 609, Fort Erie, Ontario L2A 5X3

Not valid to current subscribers of Harlequin Presents books.

Want to try two free books from another line?
Call 1-800-873-8635 or visit www.morefreebooks.com.

* Terms and prices subject to change without notice. N.Y. residents add applicable sales tax. Canadian residents will be charged applicable provincial taxes and GST. This offer is limited to one order per household. All orders subject to approval. Credit or debit balances in a customer's account(s) may be offset by any other outstanding balance owed by or to the customer. Please allow 4 to 6 weeks for delivery. Offer available while quantities last.

Your Privacy: Harlequin Books is committed to protecting your privacy. Our Privacy Policy is available online at www.eHarlequin.com or upon request from the Reader Service. From time to time we make our lists of customers available to reputable third parties who may have a product or service of interest to you. If you would prefer we not share your name and address, please check here. ☐

HP08

Don't forget Harlequin Presents EXTRA
now brings you a powerful new collection
every month featuring four books!

Be sure not to miss any of the titles in

In the Greek Tycoon's Bed,

available May 13:

THE GREEK'S
FORBIDDEN BRIDE
by Cathy Williams

THE GREEK TYCOON'S
UNEXPECTED WIFE
by Annie West

THE GREEK TYCOON'S
VIRGIN MISTRESS
by Chantelle Shaw

THE GIANNAKIS BRIDE
by Catherine Spencer